A YEAR FULL OF STORIES

WRITTEN BY ANGELA McALLISTER

ILLUSTRATED BY CHRISTOPHER CORR

Frances Lincoln
Children's Books

CONTENTS

FOR REGGIE

ABOUT THE AUTHOR

Angela McAllister is the author of over eighty books for children of all ages. Her books have been adapted for the stage, translated into many languages and have won several awards.

ABOUT THE ILLUSTRATOR

Christopher Corr is an established author/illustrator whose many books have won him international acclaim. He studied at the Royal College of Art, and now lives and works in London as an artist and tutor at Goldsmiths University.

ACKNOWLEDGEMENT

With thanks to Rebecca Eyres for her generous advice and encouragement and to Steve Westwood, Libby Langlands and Alison Macaulay for their story suggestions.

JANUARY

JANUARY 1ST
NEW YEAR'S DAY

FATHER FROST
A RUSSIAN STORY

Once there lived a man whose wife died, leaving him to care for their young daughter, Irina. As time passed, he worried that she was lonely, so he married a new wife with a daughter of her own.

"Now we shall be a family once more," he said.

But Irina's father soon realised that he'd made a terrible mistake. The stepmother was bad-tempered and hated Irina. She made her work hard, chopping wood, feeding the pigs and scrubbing the floor, while her own daughter, Nonna, lay in bed all day, eating cake. If Irina or her father dared to complain, she threw pots and pans at them both.

One winter's morning, the stepmother announced it was time for Irina to marry. "Everything is arranged," she told Irina's father. "Fetch the sleigh, take the girl into the forest and leave her by the tall pine."

"But she'll freeze in the cold!" cried Irina's father.

"She'll not wait long for her bridegroom," the stepmother promised.

Irina and her father were too afraid to protest.

Irina gathered her belongings silently. The only food she was allowed to take were peelings from the pigsty.

The stepmother watched them ride away and laughed at her cruel trick. "Goodbye and good riddance!" she cried.

Irina and her father rode deep into the forest. When they came to the tall pine he couldn't bear to leave her.

"Don't be sad, father," said Irina bravely, "hurry home or you'll be in trouble."

When he'd gone, Irina sat on a tree stump, shuddering with cold, and pulled the bundle of peelings from her pocket. Suddenly, she heard footsteps in the snow. Along came a glittering figure with a white beard, sparkling the trees with frost and showering them with icicles.

Father Frost stopped and gazed at Irina.

"Are you warm, little maid?" he asked.

"Yes, sir, I'm warm," said Irina politely, although her teeth chattered.

Father Frost stepped closer, making ice form at her feet.

"Are you still warm, little red cheeks?" he asked.

"Yes, sir, still warm," said Irina, although her toes were numb.

Father Frost stepped closer, making snowflakes fall.

"Are you still warm, little blue lips?" he asked.

Irina struggled to speak, for each breath stabbed like needles in her chest.

"Yes, sir, warm enough," she whispered.

Then Father Frost saw Irina's brave smile and took pity on her. He wrapped her in a scarlet cloak and warm blankets.

That night, Irina's father couldn't sleep. At dawn, he rode into the forest, fearing his daughter was dead. But to his joy, he found Irina alive, warmly dressed with a chest full of presents at her feet.

The stepmother was furious when they returned. "Nonna must go to the forest," she said. "She deserves richer clothes and presents than Irina!"

So, next morning, Irina's father took Nonna into the forest.

Nonna waited expectantly at the tall pine, eating cake. Before long, Father Frost appeared. He stopped and stared at Nonna.

"Are you warm, little maid?" he asked.

"Of course not!" snapped Nonna. "Give me a cloak – a fur one would suit me."

Father Frost frowned and stepped closer.

"Are you warm, little red cheeks?"

"No!" shouted Nonna. "I need a fur hat and boots too."

Father Frost stepped closer, shaking his head.

"Are you warm, little blue lips?"

"NO!" shrieked Nonna. "Are you deaf old man? Just give me the chest full of presents and make it big!"

Then Father Frost saw Nonna's greedy eyes. He raised his staff.

Next morning, the stepmother herself went into the forest. She found Nonna, pale as ice, wrapped in a cloak of frost, with nothing but a box of pine needles at her feet. She hugged her shivering daughter tight, but Nonna was so chilled that they both froze to death on the spot.

JANUARY
WINTERTIME

THE MAGIC PORRIDGE POT
A GERMAN STORY

One winter's day, Hans was walking to school when he met an old woman asking for food. Hans came from a poor family and only had a crust of bread for his lunch, but he happily shared it with the old woman, for he knew how it felt to be hungry himself.

On the way home, he met the old woman again. She handed him a little cooking pot. "This is to thank you for your kindness," she said. "Tap it and say 'Cook, little pot, cook!' and it will give you as much porridge as you wish. If you want it to stop, tap it once more and say 'Stop, little pot, stop!'" Hans thanked her and carried the pot home.

When his mother and little brother, Fritz, saw the battered old pot they thought Hans had picked up some rubbish along the path. But then he tapped it and said "Cook, little pot, cook!" Suddenly, the kitchen was filled with a delicious sweet smell and, to their amazement, the pot bubbled with thick, creamy porridge.

"Stop, little pot, stop!" said Hans, with another tap, and they all tucked in.

From that day, Hans and his family never had to go hungry again. They had porridge when-ever they wished. Sometimes they stirred in a spoonful of jam or a handful of berries. Sometimes they invited their neighbours in to share a warm meal.

Then, one morning, while Hans was at school, Fritz decided that he wanted more. His mother was outside, fetching firewood, so Fritz tapped the pot and said "Cook, little pot, cook!" Sure enough, the little pot began to fill with porridge. Fritz spooned some into his bowl and began to eat. But the pot kept cooking. He didn't notice the porridge dribbling over the top of the pot until he had licked his bowl clean. "Stop cooking pot!" he said, but the pot didn't stop. Porridge

spilled over the stove and onto the kitchen floor. Fritz began to cry and his mother came rushing in from the garden.

"What's happened?" she cried. "Stop, porridge pot, stop!" But the pot kept cooking. Porridge flooded the kitchen and flowed out through the back door. It bubbled down the path and into the street. All the cats in the village ran up to eat their fill and the dogs ran after them.

"What's happened?" cried the villagers as warm porridge oozed into their houses and shops. "Somebody stop this!" But nobody could. The children slipped and skidded and sledged in porridge, they even tried to make porridge snowmen, but soon it was too deep to play in. It filled the rooms of the houses, so that everyone had to climb out of the windows onto their rooftops. "Eat as much as you can!" cried the mayor, but it was no use, the porridge kept coming. It streamed down the road like a white lumpy river until it reached the schoolhouse.

When Hans smelt the sweet porridge he ran out of school. At once he knew what had happened. But how could he get home to put things right? A wintry gust of wind gave him an idea. The children had been making kites at school that day, so he fetched his kite and threw it into the sky. As it flew up, he grabbed onto its tail and soared high above the porridge river and over the village. When Hans reached his house he let go, and landed softly in his porridge garden. Just as he did so, the little cooking pot bobbed by. Hans tapped it. "Stop, little pot, stop!" he said and it stopped cooking at once. Hans sighed with relief.

But it took many days for people to eat their way back into their houses and nobody in that village, except Hans and his family, ever ate porridge again.

JANUARY
CHINESE NEW YEAR

KING OF THE FOREST
A CHINESE STORY

Tiger was prowling through the shadows one day when he spied Fox, sitting outside his den. Tiger smiled to himself. He leapt and pounced on Fox's tail, holding him fast.

"Let me go!" cried Fox, tugging his tail. "How dare you attack the King of the Forest?"

Tiger was taken aback. "What nonsense!" he said. "You are not the King of the Forest."

"I am," said Fox. "I'm so powerful that all the animals are afraid of me. If you don't believe it, come, and I'll show you."

Tiger was curious. He released Fox and followed him closely down the track.

They came to a herd of deer by the river. When Fox stepped forward, the deer skittered with panic and fled in all directions.

"See, I told you so," said Fox and he walked on. Tiger followed closely.

They came to a family of pigs, rooting among the trees. When Fox appeared, the pigs squealed and thundered away.

"See, I told you so," said Fox and he walked on. Tiger followed closely.

They came to a group of monkeys, sitting on a branch. When Fox stopped beneath the branch, the monkeys shrieked with fright and scrambled into the treetops.

"There, you see," said Fox, "all the animals are afraid of me."

"It's amazing but true!" Tiger agreed. "I've seen it with my own eyes. You must be the King of the Forest. Please forgive me, Your Majesty."

"I forgive you," said the crafty Fox. "But be sure not to do it again!"

Then Tiger bowed low and, with a sweep of his great tail, he slipped away into the shadows.

FEBRUARY

FEBRUARY 12TH
CANDLEMAS

THE EMPTY BARN
A LATVIAN STORY

Long ago, there was a farmer who had three sons, Valdis, Vilis and Teodors. Valdis and Vilis were tall and strong, but Teodors was young and couldn't match his brothers' strength.

One day, their father said, "Sons, this farm is doing well; our fields grow golden wheat, our meadows feed sturdy cows and our hens lay the best eggs. But the old barn has a leaky roof and rotten timbers. It's time to pull it down and build a new one."

Valdis and Vilis started work at once, pulling down the old barn.

Teodors rolled up his sleeves. "Let me help," he said, wanting to do something to make his father proud, but his brothers just laughed.

"You're not strong enough, with those little twigs you call arms," they shouted. "It takes muscles like ours to tear down a barn."

So Teodors was left to pick up any bits and pieces from the old barn that he thought might come in useful.

When they'd finished, Valdis and Vilis harnessed the horse to the wagon and went into the forest, to chop down trees for the new barn. Teodors ran after them.

"Let me chop down a tree," he begged. "Go on, let me try."

Valdis winked at Vilis.

"There's a fine, straight pine," he said. "Chop that down, little brother." Teodors grabbed the axe – but though he tugged with all his might, he wasn't even strong enough to lift it.

With a sigh, he gave up and looked after the horse instead.

Valdis and Vilis chopped down the trees they needed, lifted them onto the wagon and brought

them back to the farm. Then they began to build the new barn.

"I can help pull the rope and raise the frame," cried Teodors, but his brothers shook their heads.

"You don't weigh more than a piglet," they chuckled. "You'd make no difference at all."

Teodors tried not to look disappointed and made himself useful by shooing the chickens and ducks out of the way.

All the while, the farmer sat in his rocking chair on the porch, watching everything.

For three days Valdis and Vilis worked on the barn. Teodors wasn't strong enough to lift the beams or raise the rafters, so he fetched ladders and carried tools for his brothers. Every time Valdis needed a hammer, Teodors had one ready. Whenever Vilis ran out of nails, Teodors was standing by with a handful. They even used some of the bits and pieces he'd saved from the old barn.

Then it was time for the roof. While Valdis and Vilis sawed and hammered and heaved and puffed, Teodors made a little nesting box for the wagtails and fixed it under the eaves.

All the while, the farmer sat in his rocking chair, watching thoughtfully.

At last, the huge doors were hung and the new barn was finished.

"Sons, this is a fine barn," said the farmer. "I'm proud to see how strong and clever you

are. Whichever one of you can fill the empty barn in a day can have my rocking chair."

"We're ready for a rest!" laughed Valdis and Vilis.

Next morning, Valdis looked around for something to fill the barn. He spotted the cows in the meadow. "Those are the biggest beasts on the farm," he thought, "they'll fill the barn." So, he led the cows out of the meadow into the yard. But the cows had been enjoying sweet grass in the meadow, they didn't want to go into a barn. Valdis pushed and shoved. He dragged them by the horns and dug his heels in hard, but as soon as he got one cow through the door, another barged out again. All day he heaved the stubborn cows into the barn and chased after the ones that escaped. But by the end of the day he finally had them all inside.

"Well, Valdis," said his father, "you have filled the barn from wall to wall, but you haven't filled it up to the roof."

Valdis sighed wearily and led the cows back to the meadow.

Next morning, Vilis headed for the fields. "We've grown plenty of wheat this year," he thought. "That should fill the empty barn." So he loaded up the wagon with sheaves of wheat and took it back to the yard. As he heaved the wheat in and out it scratched and tickled and poked his ears, but back and forth he went, hour after hour, until, at last the fields were empty.

"Well, Vilis," said his father, "you've filled the barn to the roof, but not from wall to wall."

Vilis frowned and mopped his brow, then he began to carry the wheat out again. By the time he had emptied the barn, it was dark.

"Your turn tomorrow, Teodors," said his father. But Teodors shook his head.

"No, I'm ready now, Father," he said with a mysterious smile. "I won't take long."

Teodors's father and brothers were puzzled. They watched as he walked into the barn and took something out of his pocket — it was a bundle of candles that he'd saved from the old barn. Teodors placed the candles around the barn and lit them carefully. One by one, a dozen little flames flickered and then they grew, shining brightly and filling the whole barn with golden light.

"Clever boy!" cried his father. "You've filled every inch of the empty barn, from wall to wall and floor to roof. The rocking chair is yours!"

Teodors grinned proudly. "You keep it, Father," he said, "I haven't got time to sit on a rocking chair. I'm going to work hard to grow as tall and strong as Valdis and Vilis!"

Then the barn was filled again, with the laughter of the farmer and his three sons.

"It might take you a while to grow as tall and strong as your brothers, Teodors," said his father, "but you'll always be the cleverest!"

FEBRUARY 14TH
VALENTINE'S DAY

THE FROG PRINCE
A GERMAN STORY

Long ago and far away, there lived a lonely princess. One morning, the princess wandered beyond the palace garden into the wood, throwing and catching her golden ball. Suddenly, a stag leapt across her path and she missed her catch. The golden ball bounced off a log and fell into a deep, dark pool.

The princess stared into the water, but she couldn't see even a glint of gold. She began to cry. As her tears dropped into the pool, two glassy eyes blinked up at her. Out of the water clambered a frog.

"Ugh!" the princess shuddered. She hated slimy creatures. But, to her surprise, the frog opened his mouth to speak.

"Why are you sad, Princess?" he asked.

The princess was so astonished that she forgot to be afraid. "I've lost my golden ball," she answered.

The frog hopped a little nearer. "I can fetch it for you," he said.

The princess dried her eyes. "I promise you a ruby as big as my thumb if you bring it to me," she said.

The frog laughed. "I don't need a ruby," he chuckled. "But if you promise to love me and let me sit at your table and eat from your plate, sip from your cup and sleep on your pillow, then I'll fetch your golden ball."

"I promise whatever you wish," said the princess, for the ball was a favourite present from her father. And so the frog jumped into the pool with a splash.

Before long, the princess saw something gleam in the murky water and up came the frog with her ball in his mouth.

FEBRUARY

"Thank you!" she cried happily and before the frog could catch his breath she slipped the ball safely into her pocket and hurried away home to the palace.

"Wait, take me with you!" shouted the frog, but the princess was already too far away to hear.

The next evening, the princess was having supper when she heard a tiny croak at the foot of her chair. She looked down and gasped.

"What's the matter?" cried the king.

"It's a horrid old water-splasher!" exclaimed the queen.

The frog made a bow. "Remember your promise, princess," he said. "I've travelled all night and all day to find you."

"What does this mean?" asked the king. The princess explained how the frog had fetched her ball in return for a promise. "Then you must keep your promise," insisted the King.

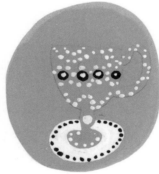

The princess looked at the frog's warty skin and webbed feet. "I can't bear to pick him up, Father," she said, but the king only gave her a frown. So the princess laid a spoon on the floor and let the frog hop on board, then she lifted him onto the table.

"Now, you must let me eat from your plate, Princess," said the frog. "I'm hungry after diving to the bottom of the deep, dark pool." The princess was hungry herself, but she pushed her plate towards him.

When the frog saw her fine food he shook his head.

"Frogs eat slugs and worms," he said. So the king ordered the footman to fetch slugs and worms from the garden and put them on the princess's plate.

"Thank you," said the frog politely. He opened his mouth and shot out his tongue.

"I feel quite sick," said the princess, turning away, and she refused to eat another morsel.

"Now, you must let me drink from your cup," said the frog. "I'm thirsty after carrying your heavy ball from the bottom of the pool." The princess hesitated, but she caught the king's eye. So she tipped her cup until the frog could hold it with his tiny fingers. He gulped noisily, splashing her drink on the tablecloth.

"I'll get warts if I share that cup!" cried the princess, so she went thirsty. When the frog had finished eating and drinking he bowed to the king and queen, stretched his skinny legs and yawned. "Now, you must let me sleep on your pillow, Princess," he said. "I'm tired after travelling all night and all day." The princess didn't want to carry the cold, damp creature to her bedchamber, but she knew it was useless to protest.

"Hop onto my shoulder, Frog," said the princess and although he smelt of pond-weed she tried not to flinch. "At least I won't have to look at him when I'm asleep," she thought, "and tomorrow I'll have kept all my promises and he must leave."

The princess had a big bed; she let the frog sleep on one side and kept herself as far away from him as she could.

"Goodnight, Princess," said the frog, wearily.

"Goodnight, Frog," she sighed and shut her eyes tight.

In the morning, when the princess awoke, the frog was sitting on her pillow, looking very unhappy.

"Why are you sad, Frog?" she asked.

"You let me sit at your table and eat from your plate, sip from your cup and sleep on your pillow," said the frog, "but do you love me, Princess?"

As he spoke these words, the princess caught sight of her golden ball on the shelf. She thought of how the frog had dived to the bottom of the deep, dark pool for her; how he'd travelled all day and all night to find her; how she had never slept so well, with him asleep beside her.

"You think I'm a horrid creature," said the frog sadly.

"It's not true!" cried the princess. Suddenly she no longer saw his warty skin or his webbed feet, she saw only his gentle eyes and his kind heart. "I was foolish and blind." She reached across the pillow and kissed his tiny green head.

All at once, there was a flash of light and the frog disappeared. Standing before her was a handsome young prince.

"I've been under the spell of a wicked witch," he said. "At last, your love has set me free!"

The king and the queen came running. "What happened?" they cried. "Who is this?"

"It's old water-splasher!" laughed the prince.

The princess was so astonished that she couldn't speak. She leapt out of bed and flung her arms around the prince's neck.

"Dear Frog!" she sighed. "Dearest Frog Prince!"

"Thank you for keeping your promise, my love," he said.

And the golden ball tumbled off the shelf and rolled at their happy feet.

FEBRUARY

FEBRUARY 14TH
VALENTINE'S DAY

THE MOLE'S WEDDING
A KOREAN STORY

By the river Kingin stood a great stone statue, so tall that clouds often gathered around its head. Nearby lived a mole and his wife, who had a daughter they loved more than anything in the world.

One day, a handsome young mole came to ask if he could marry their daughter. The daughter liked him at once, but her proud father shook his head. "You are only a mole," he said. "Our daughter is most precious, she deserves to marry the greatest being in the world."

The daughter was sad to see the young mole turned away.

"Who is the greatest being in the world, Father?" she asked.

Her father gazed up into the sky. "Nothing is greater than the sun," he said, so he climbed up to the top of the statue to talk to the sun.

"O dazzling, magnificent Sun, greatest being in the world," said the mole, "will you do us the honour of marrying our precious daughter?"

The sun dimmed his light a little. "Alas, I am not as great as you think, Mole," he said. "Cloud can hide my face for many days. He is greater than I am."

Mole bowed to the sun, then he asked Crane to fly him up into the sky.

"O vast, pearly Cloud, greatest being in the world," said the mole, "will you do us the honour of marrying our precious daughter?"

Cloud billowed and sighed. "Sadly, I'm not as great as you imagine, Mole," he said. "Wind has the power to blow me east and west. He is greater than I am."

Mole bowed to Cloud, then he asked Crane to fly him to the mountain peak.

"O wild, racing Wind, greatest being in the world," said the mole, "will you do us the honour of marrying our precious daughter?"

Wind whistled and roared. "I wish I was the greatest, Mole," he said, "but down by the river is a stone statue, who will not be moved, no matter how hard I blow. He is greater than I am."

Mole bowed to the wind, then he hurried down the mountain to the statue below.

"O ancient, towering Statue, greatest being in the world," said the mole, "will you do us the honour of marrying our precious daughter?"

The statue smiled wisely. "Nothing is great forever, Mole," he said. "There is a creature who burrows through the ground beneath me and will topple me over one day. He is greater than I am."

Mole bowed to the statue and hurried away to search beneath the stone for the greatest being in the world. There, to his surprise, he found the handsome young mole who had wanted to marry his daughter.

"Forgive me," said the mole. "I thought you were not great enough to marry my daughter, but I have travelled to the top of the statue and up into the sky, from the mountain peak down to our dear, dark earth, to learn that you are, indeed, the greatest being in the world. Would you still consider doing us the honour of marrying our precious daughter?"

The young mole laughed. "That would make me the happiest being in the world!" he said. "But she must choose for herself."

The mole's daughter was very relieved to hear that she wasn't to marry the sun and when she met the handsome young mole again it wasn't long before her mother was preparing a feast for their wedding.

On the day of the wedding, Wind blew Cloud away from Sun so he could shine down upon the happy couple, until it was time to set below the river Kingin and let the stars come out.

"What a perfect match," said the bride's father proudly, "the greatest, happiest bridegroom for the most precious daughter in the world!"

FEBRUARY
SHROVE TUESDAY

THE RUNAWAY PANCAKE
A GERMAN STORY

One morning, a woman mixed up some batter and fried a huge pancake for her seven children.

"I'm the eldest," said the biggest boy, "I'll have the first bite."

"I need to grow," said the smallest, "I should have the first bite."

"I stirred the batter," cried his sister, "I deserve the first bite!" All the children began to argue.

When it heard this, the pancake took fright. It wriggled and flapped and jumped right out of the pan. The children were too busy quarrelling to notice the pancake roll across the kitchen floor, out of the back door and down the hill.

"Catch that pancake!" cried their mother and all the children ran after it. But the pancake was too fast to catch.

At the bottom of the hill it passed a hare.

"Stop," called the hare, "you look good to eat!"

"I've run away from seven squabbling children and I'll run away from you," laughed the pancake and on it rolled.

"Stop," bleated a goat, "you smell tasty!"

"I've run away from seven squabbling children and a hungry hare and I'll run away from you," laughed the pancake and on it rolled.

"Stop," barked a fox, "you'd make a fine meal!"

"I've run away from seven squabbling children, a hungry hare and a greedy goat and I'll run away from you," laughed the pancake and on it rolled.

The pancake came to a river and had to stop.

Along trotted a pig. "Let me carry you across the river," he said kindly.

"Thank you," said the pancake and rolled onto his snout. Then the pig swam half way across, tossed the pancake into the air and swallowed it whole!

MARCH

MARCH 1ST
ST DAVID'S DAY

MARCH

GELERT THE HOUND
A WELSH STORY

In the days when wolves roamed the mountains and valleys of Wales, there lived a prince called Llewelyn, who had a brave greyhound named Gelert. Llewelyn had raised Gelert from a pup and the faithful dog never left his side, unless they went hunting together, when no other hound was as swift or tireless in the chase.

Llewelyn also had a baby son. The child's mother had died and so Llewelyn always kept him close by, with a nurse to care for his needs.

One day, Prince Llewelyn heard that a wolf was taking young lambs from the farms nearby, so he gathered some men and rode to his hunting lodge. There, the nurse settled the baby in a cradle by the fire and Prince Llewelyn kissed him goodbye. Then the hunting party set off, with Gelert leading the hounds.

The prince and his hunters rode all morning in search of the wolf, but no matter how far the hounds roamed, they couldn't pick up its scent.

After a while, the prince noticed that Gelert was missing. He took up his horn, which always brought Gelert bounding back to him, and blew a note across the valley, loud and clear. Once, twice, three times he blew, but to his surprise, the dog didn't return.

Hour after hour, the hunters searched for the wolf and Prince Llewelyn called for his beloved hound. As daylight faded, without sight or sound of either, he feared that Gelert had found the wolf and lost the fight.

With a heavy heart, the prince called off the chase and headed home to the hunting lodge. His only comfort was the thought of seeing his son.

MARCH

However, when he arrived at the lodge, to his delight, Gelert stood in the doorway.

"There you are! Why did you leave me, old friend?" laughed the prince, leaping off his horse. But Gelert didn't come bounding up to lick his master's hand. The prince saw at once that something was wrong. Gelert gazed up at him with loving eyes, but his tail hung low and his nose and paws were stained red. Gelert turned away and staggered unsteadily into the lodge.

Prince Llewelyn's heart was filled with dread. He rushed inside and found the cradle overturned and torn bedclothes, splattered with blood, strewn across the floor. His son was nowhere to be seen.

"What have you done!" cried the prince in horror. In a desperate moment of grief he drew his sword and plunged it into the dog's side.

Gelert fell at his master's feet with a whimper.

As if in answer, the prince heard a muffled cry. He lifted the cradle and there was his son, lying safely beneath. Tears streamed down Prince Llewelyn's cheeks as he held him tight. The nurse came running in.

"O Sire," she gasped, "I thought the wolf had taken him!"

Then the prince turned and saw the body of a huge wolf, lying behind the door, bearing the wounds of a terrible fight. At once, he realised what his brave, faithful hound had done. He handed the baby to the nurse and hugged his beloved companion.

"Forgive me, Gelert, forgive me," he cried, "I should never have doubted you." But it was too late. Gelert gently licked the prince's hand and died in his master's arms.

Next morning, Prince Llewelyn buried his old friend and laid a stone at the grave. To this day, that place still bears the honour of his name – Beth Gelert.

MARCH 3RD
WORLD WILDLIFE DAY

MARCH

THE BIRD WIFE
AN INUIT STORY

Itajung was unhappy because he could not find a wife, so he packed his belongings onto his sled and left home to search elsewhere. After many days travelling across ice and snow, he came to the land of the birds. There, he found a lake in which many geese were swimming, and on the shore stood as many pairs of tiny boots. Itajung stole a pair and hid them in his coat.

When the geese came out of the water, they found one pair of boots was missing. At once they took fright and flew away. But one of the flock remained.

Itajung stepped out of his hiding place. "I will give you your boots," he said, "if you will be my wife."

"It is not my nature to be your wife," said the goose.

"Very well," said Itajung and he turned away. But the goose called him back.

"It is not my nature," she said, "but I'll be your wife if you return my boots." So Itajung set the boots before her, and when she put them on she was changed into a woman.

Itajung and his wife travelled from the land of the birds to a village by the sea, as she wished to live by water. There, they soon had a son.

Itajung earned the respect of his neighbours, for he was the best whale hunter in the village. However, his wife would never help the other women cut up the whale and carry the blubber to their homes.

"My food is not from the sea," she told Itajung, "my food is from the land. I will not touch the meat of the whale."

"You must eat," insisted Itajung, "it will fill your stomach." But his wife only cried and walked by the shore alone.

Itajung didn't notice that she began to collect feathers along the shore. One day, when she had enough, she fixed them between her fingers and the fingers of her son, and they were both turned into geese and flew away.

When Itajung saw his wife and son fly beyond the clouds his heart was broken. He no longer wanted to hunt or eat. He harnessed his dogs to the sled and set off to search for them.

Itajung travelled across ice and snow for many months, until he came to a lake, where a man was chopping wood. Each wood chip that flew from the man's axe turned into a salmon and leapt into the lake.

"Have you seen a woman and a boy?" asked Itajung.

"Yes," said the man. "She lives on the island in the middle of the lake, but she has a new husband now." Itajung stared across the water in dismay.

"I must see her," he said, "but I have no kayak."

"I'll help you," said the man. He gave Itajung the backbone of a salmon and told him to lay it in the water.

Itajung did as he was told, and the backbone of the salmon turned into a fine kayak which carried him across the lake.

When he reached the shore he saw the child and his mother, outside their house.

"Come home," pleaded Itajung. "You are my wife."

"It is not my nature to be any man's wife, Itajung," said the woman. Her new husband appeared with a box in his hands. Out of the box flew a thousand feathers which stuck fast to them. Then the woman, the child and her husband were transformed into geese and flew away, leaving Itajung standing alone.

MARCH

MARCH
PURIM

THE BLUE COAT
A JEWISH STORY

David's grandad was a tailor. When David was small, he liked to watch his grandad cut the cloth and stitch the pieces together, to make wonderful clothes.

One winter's day, David noticed some blue cloth on the shelf.

"That's just enough to make you a coat," said Grandad. So he cut up the blue cloth and made David a warm coat. Then they went out to search for animal tracks in the snow.

David loved the blue coat, but next winter it was too small.

"I can make something of that," said Grandad and he cut up the coat and made David a blue jacket. Then they went to the park and Grandad taught him how to ride a bike.

David loved his blue jacket, but eventually it worn thin.

"I can make something of that," said Grandad and he cut up the jacket and made David a blue cap. Then he took him down to the river to learn how to fish.

David loved his blue cap, but one day a dog chewed it and left only a scrap.

"I can make something of that," said Grandad and he made a blue button and sewed it onto David's shirt. Then he asked David to put away his needles and pins.

As time passed, the button frayed until all that was left was a thread.

"That's the end of our blue cloth," said David sadly.

"No, no," said Grandad, "you can make something of that. Tell me about the blue coat."

So David told Grandad about all the clothes he'd made for him and the wonderful things they'd done together.

Grandad smiled. "You see," he said, "there was enough blue cloth to make a story!"

MARCH 17TH
ST PATRICK'S DAY

MARCH

THE POT OF GOLD
AN IRISH STORY

Donal O'Malley was walking down the lane one morning when he heard the sound of hammering, tap-tap-tap! He peered over a gate into a cabbage field, and saw a tiny man in a pointed hat and a leather apron, sitting cross-legged, mending a shoe.

Donal's heart skipped a beat. "A leprechaun! What a piece of luck!" he thought. Everyone knew that if you found a leprechaun he had to tell you where he'd hidden his pot of gold.

"Now, Donal," he said to himself excitedly, "here's a chance to be rich! Keep calm, don't give the little fellow a fright. If you keep your sharp eyes on him he can't escape."

The leprechaun stopped his hammering as soon as Donal opened the gate.

"I see it's going to rain," said the leprechaun, although there wasn't a cloud in sky. "Will you be hurrying to take the shortcut through the other field?"

"No, no," said Donal. "Here is where I want to be."

"Then I'd thank you to shut the gate for the draft," said the leprechaun. But Donal wasn't going to be tricked into turning around.

"Now I've found you, I want your pot of gold," he said.

The leprechaun scratched his beard thoughtfully. "Well, well, don't be so hasty," he said with a frown. "I'll take you to my pot of gold alright, but you'll not be walking far in those worn old boots – why don't I make you a new pair before we start?"

Donal reached down and grabbed the leprechaun. "I don't need any boots!" he said impatiently.

"Let me go!" squeaked the little man. He kicked and wriggled and walloped Donal with his tiny hammer. "Stop your squeezing, or I'll have no breath for telling you where it is."

"Then promise you'll show me and no mischief!" said Donal and the leprechaun agreed.

As soon as he was on his feet, the leprechaun straightened his hat and set off across the cabbage field. Donal was surprised at how fast his tiny legs carried him and watched every step in case he ducked out of sight.

When they reached the middle of the field the leprechaun stopped and pointed at a cabbage.

"Here it is," he said. "All my life's treasure, all my shiny gold, it's buried under here. You just have to dig it up."

Donal could almost hear the jingle of gold coins in his hands.

"Of course," muttered the leprechaun, "you'll be needing a spade."

Donal realised he was in a fix! If he went home to fetch a spade, he'd never find that cabbage again. Then he had an idea. He unknotted the red handkerchief that he'd wrapped around his neck that morning and tied it around the cabbage.

"Promise me you won't touch that handkerchief while I go home for a spade?" he said sternly to the leprechaun.

"Oh no, no, I'll not lay a finger on it," said the leprechaun, lighting up his pipe. "You can trust me, honest you can."

So Donal rushed home to fetch a spade.

As he hurried back up the lane, Donal thought of all the wonderful things he was going to buy with his pot of gold. "You'll never have to do another day's work, Donal old boy," he laughed to himself. But when he reached the field he stopped at the gate and stared... every cabbage as far as the eye could see was tied with a red handkerchief!

Donal's heart sank. The crafty leprechaun was nowhere to be seen, but from far away came the sound of a tiny chuckle and a tap-tap-tap!

MARCH

MARCH 22ND
WORLD WATER DAY

MARCH

TIDDALIK, THE THIRSTY FROG
AN INDIGENOUS AUSTRALIAN STORY

Long ago, in Dreamtime, when the world was still being made, there lived a small frog called Tiddalik. The hot sun made him thirsty, so Tiddalik hopped down to the waterhole for a drink.

Tiddalik drank and drank until the waterhole was dry, but still he felt thirsty. So, he drank all the water in the creek, then all the billabongs and the swamps and the rivers and lagoons – until there wasn't a drop of water left in the land. After he'd finished, Tiddalik's belly was as huge as a mountain and he was too heavy to hop anywhere.

When the other animals grew thirsty there was nothing for them to drink. They pleaded with Tiddalik to give them some water, but he kept his mouth firmly shut.

"Let's make him laugh," suggested Wombat.

"Good idea," said Kookaburra and she told some jokes. But Tiddalik didn't even smile.

Koala stood on her head, Echidna made funny faces and Lizard danced a silly dance – but still Tiddalik sat with his lips closed tight.

Last to try was Kangaroo, who boxed with his shadow, thump, thump, thump! The thumping disturbed Platypus who'd been sleeping nearby.

"Who woke me up?" she said, snapping her beak. Tiddalik stared in surprise, he'd never seen such a weird looking creature.

Platypus banged her tail and tapped her webbed feet crossly. "Well, what's going on?" The angrier she got, the more ridiculous she looked.

At last, Tiddalik couldn't help himself, he opened his mouth to laugh.

"Watch out!" cried Wombat.

Out gushed a great flood, filling the waterholes and creeks, the billabongs and swamps and lagoons; plenty enough for all the animals to drink.

32

APRIL

APRIL 1ST
APRIL FOOLS' DAY

APRIL

RABBIT AND CRAB
A MAYAN STORY

Rabbit and his friend, Crab, decided to grow some carrots. They worked together, digging the ground, planting seeds and watering them until the shoots began to grow. Then they weeded the carrot patch and watched, week by week, until it was time to harvest the crop.

When they had dug up the sweet juicy carrots and cut off their green tops, Rabbit carefully made two piles.

"You have the big pile, dear Crab," he said, "and I'll take the small one."

Crab looked at the two piles – the biggest one was all carrot tops.

"Thank you, Rabbit, old friend," he said, "but I have a fairer way. Why don't I divide the piles in half and you choose which you want. Or, you divide the piles and I choose?"

Rabbit suspected that Crab was trying to confuse him. "I've got a better plan," he said. "Let's go to the big cactus over there and race back here – the one who wins gets the carrots and the one who loses gets the tops?"

Crab thought for a moment, then he smiled at Rabbit. "All right," he said, "that seems fair."

So Rabbit and Crab walked over to the big cactus together.

Rabbit hopped along with great confidence. "You are such a good friend, Crab, that if you win I'm happy to give you all the carrots and all the tops too," he said.

"Well, thank you," said Crab, scuttling as fast as he could to keep up. "That's most kind."

"And as you are a little slower than me, you can start ahead," added Rabbit, for he had no doubt that he would win the race and soon be munching on the pile of crisp, juicy carrots himself.

APRIL

But Crab wouldn't agree. "No, no, you are being very generous, Rabbit, you should start ahead," he said. "I insist."

Rabbit chuckled to himself. "Well, I gave him a chance!" he thought, so he didn't argue about it.

When they reached the big cactus, Rabbit and Crab turned and faced the piles of carrots and green tops in the distance.

"May the best man win," said Crab.

Rabbit took ten paces forward. He didn't notice that Crab had seized his tail with his claws and was hanging on tight.

"Ready, steady, GO!" shouted Rabbit and he bounded away.

Rabbit ran like the wind and reached the carrots in no time. As he turned to see how far Crab was behind him, Crab opened his claws and dropped right on top of the pile.

"Where are you, old friend?" shouted Rabbit, pretending to be concerned.

"Oh, I was here long ago," said a voice behind him.

Rabbit nearly jumped out of his skin. He spun round in surprise. There before him was Crab, waving a triumphant carrot. "But… but… how… what?" stammered Rabbit.

"The best man won!" said Crab. "But I don't want you to go hungry, Rabbit, old friend. I can be generous too. You take as many of those carrot tops as you wish."

Rabbit went home, feeling cross that he'd been tricked, but he never worked out how he'd been beaten by a slow, scuttling crab.

APRIL

THE BASKET OF EGGS
A CANADIAN STORY

King Winter reigned over the cold, dark months of the year. He sat on a frosty throne in his palace of ice, commanding snow to fall and gusts of chilling wind to whistle across the land. While he reigned, nothing could grow in the frozen earth and everything seemed lifeless.

One day, a glimmer of sunlight danced on the icicles hanging from the palace roof. King Winter began to feel sleepy.

"Spring has woken up," he sighed with a yawn, "I can hear her footsteps." Slowly he began to melt, drip by drip, until all that was left of him was a pool of water.

Now, where King Winter had reigned, Spring walked. She was a young girl with long yellow hair and violet eyes. Wherever she passed, snow and ice melted, filling the rivers and streams. Wherever she gazed, grass grew and flowers sprung up, dancing in warm breezes that flowed from her hair.

The world was full of joy and hope. In the woods, the animals gathered to prepare for Easter.

"Who will carry the basket of Easter eggs to the village children this year?" asked Speckled Hen. "It's a heavy load for me to manage."

"Let me carry the basket," said Weasel. "It will be safe with me."

"We know how much you like eating eggs," said the other animals in alarm. "The basket would soon be empty!"

Bear stepped forward. "I've had a good winter sleep," he said. "I'll carry the eggs."

"Oh no," cried everyone, "you'll frighten the children! We need somebody gentle."

Speckled Hen noticed the white rabbit. "Children always love to see you," she said.

APRIL

"Will you carry the basket of eggs?" Rabbit agreed. "So everything is settled," said Speckled Hen.

But the world was not yet ready for Easter.

In the meadow, the flowers were deciding which one of them should be the Easter flower.

"Choose me!" called Briar Rose from the hedge.

"No," said the other flowers, "you are too thorny."

"How about Violet?" suggested Daisy, but Violet was too shy.

"The white Lily should be the Easter flower," she said. "She is as pure as the heart of Jesus." So the Lily was chosen.

But the world was still not ready for Easter.

The birds had flocked together to choose which one of them should sing on Easter morning.

"Obviously it should be me," said Crow. "I have the loudest voice, so everyone will hear me!"

The other birds chirruped amongst themselves. "Your voice may be loud, Crow, but it's very harsh," they said.

"Then choose me," suggested Sparrow. "Everybody loves a chirpy Sparrow." But nobody wanted chirping for Easter, they wanted a fine song.

"Let's ask Robin," said Blackbird, "he has a musical voice and his breast is red like the blood of Jesus."

Robin was proud to be chosen. "What tree shall I sing from on Easter morning?" he said.

"You can stand in my boughs," said the oak. But the cross Jesus carried was made of oak.

"You can sit on my needles," said the pine.

"No, you're much too prickly," said Robin. He flew over to the willow. "May I sing from your branches?" he asked. "It was a willow that wept to see Jesus suffer." Willow humbly agreed.

Next morning, all the village children received eggs from Rabbit's basket. On the way to church, they heard Robin sing from the willow tree and before the altar they saw white lilies standing tall. The world was ready at last to celebrate Easter, full of hope and joy, and everyone sang, "Hallelujah!"

APRIL 7TH
WORLD HEALTH DAY

APRIL

HOW THE BEAR CLAN LEARNT TO HEAL
AN IROQUOIS STORY

Three young hunters were running home one evening, when a rabbit jumped out ahead of them and sat in the middle of the trail. The hunters stopped. They'd already caught plenty of game, but each one reached for his bow, plucked an arrow from his quiver and shot at the rabbit. To their surprise, the arrows returned without a spot of blood.

As they reached for a second arrow, the rabbit disappeared. In its place stood a bent old man.

"I am sick," said the old man weakly. "Help me find food and a place to rest." The young hunters didn't want to be bothered by the old man. Ignoring his plea, they put away their arrows and ran on down the trail. They didn't notice the old man turn and follow.

When he reached the hunters' settlement, the old man saw many lodges. In front of each lodge was a skin hanging on a pole. This was the sign of the clan within.

The old man stopped at the lodge of the Wolf clan and asked the elder woman for shelter, but she wouldn't let him in. "We don't want any sickness here," she said. So he shuffled on.

The young women at the Beaver lodge insisted they had no food to share. The Turtle clan and Deer clan both sent him away. The old man asked for help at the sign of the Hawk, Snipe and Heron, but everyone shook their heads.

Night fell and the air grew cold. At last he came to the lodge of the Bear Clan. When the

APRIL

Bear Clan mother saw the sick old man she lifted the blanket at her door and welcomed him inside. She gave him a bowl of warm corn mash and spread soft skins for him to rest on. The old man was grateful. The next day, he told her what herbs to fetch from the woods to make him well, and soon he was healed.

The old man stayed with the Bear Clan mother, but a few days later he became sick again. As before, she cared for him. He told her what roots and leaves to use for medicine and she made him well.

Many times the old man fell ill; once with a fever, another time with pain, then a rash and a cough. Each time, he instructed her about the flowers and plants to use for his condition and she listened and learnt well. Before long, she knew more about healing than anyone in all the clans.

One evening, as they sat together under the stars, the old man gave the clan mother thanks. "I was sent to earth by the Great Spirit to teach people the secrets of healing," he said. "You were the only one who showed pity and welcomed me at your fireside. Now I have taught you how to use plants and roots to heal the sick and from this day all the other clans will come to learn from the Bear Clan how to heal, and the Bear Clan will be the greatest and the strongest of all."

Then the clan mother was filled with joy. She gazed up at the sky and thanked the Great Spirit for his precious gift. But when she turned again to the old man he had disappeared. All she saw was a rabbit running away down the trail.

APRIL 23RD
ST GEORGE'S DAY

THE GLASS KNIGHT
AN ENGLISH STORY

A farmer and his son were passing a wood on their way to market one morning when they noticed many trees were dead.

The farmer was puzzled. "Those trees were fine yesterday," he said, so he stopped his cart and climbed down to look. The son followed. Inside the wood there was an eerie silence, every bush and tree was shrivelled and black.

"There's something dark and dangerous here, Son," whispered the farmer. As he spoke, they saw a flash of yellow and glimpsed the back of a winged creature, with cockerel's feet and a serpent's tail.

"Run, Father!" cried the son, but his father was fixed to the spot. The creature spun round and gazed at him with blood-red eyes and in an instant the farmer dropped down dead.

The farmer's son ran home to the village, so terrified he could hardly speak. When the villagers heard what had happened, the bravest men set off at once after the beast.

But by nightfall they hadn't returned. Everyone gathered in church to decide what to do.

"What monster can strike living things dead with its eyes?" they asked. Nobody had ever heard of such a beast. Then the wise woman of the village spoke.

"I fear it is a Basilisk," she said darkly, "a creature with the head and claws of a cockerel, the tail of a serpent and the wings of a bat. Its breath can break stone and its touch is poison, but most terrifying are its blood-red eyes that kill anything at a glance."

The villagers listened in stunned silence. "Is there nothing we can do?" they asked, but the wise woman shook her head. The villagers hurried home, locked their doors

and closed their shutters. Nobody slept a wink.

The next day, a wandering knight rode into the village and stopped at the inn to rest. When he heard about the Basilisk he felt sorry for the frightened villagers. "I've faced many dangers," he said. "I promise I shall rid you of this terrible beast." So the innkeeper sent him to talk to the wise woman.

The knight listened to all the wise woman told him. "Does the Basilisk ever shut its eyes?" he asked.

"Only to drink," she said, "but his ears are so keen you'll never catch him unawares!"

That evening, the knight sat thinking in his room at the inn. He realised that his bravery alone would not be enough to defeat the beast. How could he keep his vow and save the village? Glancing up, he caught sight of his worried face in the mirror above the fireplace. Suddenly, he understood why the Basilisk shut its eyes

to drink and it gave him an idea.

Early the next morning the knight rode away.

"Who can blame him," sighed the innkeeper, and the villagers sadly agreed.

But two days later there was a great commotion as the knight returned in sparkling armour, covered with scales of crystal glass. Even his visor was a shining mirror. Everyone cheered as he walked through the village and on into the wood.

Deep in its lair, the Basilisk heard the knight approach. It uncurled its tail, stretched its claws and strutted out to meet its prey.

Then the glass knight stepped forward.

The Basilisk raised its blood-red eyes — and saw a thousand reflections of itself! With a shriek of horror it turned away, but too late — its wings began to shrivel and its skin turned black. With an angry thrash of its tail, the Basilisk fell dead to the ground.

APRIL

APRIL 23RD
ST GEORGE'S DAY

APRIL

THE SHOEMAKER AND THE DRAGON

A POLISH STORY

King Krak lived in a castle on the top of Wawel Hill, high above the winding river Vistula, but his kingdom was not a happy one. Down below, in a cave at the bottom of the hill, lived a terrifying, fire-belching dragon called Smok Wawelski.

Smok Wawelski struck fear into the heart of everyone in the land. He stole cattle from the farms and set fire to houses, and when people rushed out in alarm, he'd snatch them up in his claws and take them back to his lair.

Brave men came from far and wide to fight Smok Wawelski, but before they could get close enough to throw a spear or thrust a sword in his side, the blistering flames of the dragon's fiery breath would burn them to a cinder.

King Krak was deeply troubled. "People are too afraid to leave their houses or work in the fields," he told his daughter, Princess Wanda. "There must be someone who can rid us of this curse."

"I wish I could fight the dragon myself, Father," said the princess. "But maybe there is a way I can help. I shall offer my hand in marriage to anyone who can defeat him."

So, the following day, a proclamation was read throughout the land, offering the hand of the princess in marriage to anyone who could put an end to Smok Wawelski.

Soon, many young men arrived, each with a daring plan to defeat the dragon and marry the

44

princess, but despite their valour, every one met the same grisly fate.

Meanwhile, a clever young shoemaker in the town had been watching the dragon come and go from his workshop window. He had no sword or spear, no armour to protect him from the dragon's claws, but he had a bold idea.

He waited until he saw Smok Wawelski fly from his cave, then he ventured out to buy some sulphur.

"Handle this with care," said the miner who sold it to him. "It's fiery stuff!"

Next, the shoemaker bought three dead sheep and filled their bellies with the sulphur. Then he stitched them up and heaved them into his cart.

Keeping a sharp eye on the sky in case the dragon appeared, the shoemaker rode up to Smok Wawelski's cave and pushed the sheep off the cart, right in front of the entrance. Then he hurried out of sight and hid behind a rock.

The shoemaker didn't have to wait long before he heard a terrifying roar and the dragon returned. Smok Wawelski stopped outside the cave, sniffed the sheep and licked his smouldering

APRIL

lips. Although his claws were red with blood, he was still hungry. He devoured the sheep, hooves, horns and all, then went into his cave to rest.

The shoemaker waited. Moments later, Smok Wawelski flew out again, puffing and wheezing, burning with fiery sulphur inside. He rushed down to the river and began to gulp water as fast as he could. But no matter how much he drank, he felt as though he'd swallowed a volcano. On and on and on he drank, swelling bigger and bigger and bigger until, with a deafening shriek, he exploded!

At once, people came running down to the river. "The shoemaker saved us!" they cheered.

There was much celebration on Wawel Hill that night and it was soon followed by the happy wedding of Princess Wanda and the clever shoemaker.

And if you visit Wawel Hill, high above the winding river Vistula, you may see the old king's castle and the dragon's cave for yourself.

APRIL

MAY 1ST
MAY DAY

MAY
❋ ❋ ❋

THE CRACKED POT
AN INDIAN STORY

Every day, the water-bearer walked down to the stream, with two large pots hanging from a pole across his shoulders, to fetch water for his master's house.

When he first began, he used to run down the steep path with a whistle, but that was many years ago. Now he was old and bent, his shoulders ached, his legs were weak and one of the pots had a crack. It was time for a younger man to take over the task.

On his last day of work, the old water-bearer emptied his pots in the kitchen and went out to sit in the shade.

To his surprise, the cracked pot spoke.

"Forgive me for disturbing your rest," said the pot, "but may I ask one question?"

The water-bearer smiled. "I will answer you as best I can, old friend," he said.

"You know I've been cracked for many years," said the pot, "I always arrive at the master's house half empty. So, why have you never replaced me?"

"Let's take one last walk to the stream together," said the water-bearer, "and then I will answer your question."

The water-bearer filled the pots at the stream and began to walk back, with the cracked pot dripping as always. Halfway, he stopped and sat on a rock.

"Now," he said to the cracked pot, "have you noticed the flowers that only grow on your side of the path? I planted them because I knew you would water them every day."

He sighed happily. "Thanks to you, I've been able to enjoy beautiful flowers every spring. To me, your flaw is a blessing. That, my friend, is why I never replaced you."

MAY
SPRINGTIME

SPRING AND AUTUMN
A JAPANESE STORY

Once there was a princess so beautiful that she was called Dear Delight of the World. Princes, warriors and even gods came from near and far, to gaze at the princess and offer precious gifts. Each one hoped he could win her as his bride.

The princess listened politely to her admirers, but none of them ever stirred her heart. To their dismay, she would silently shake her head and send them away.

One day, the God of Autumn came to the palace. He was handsome, brave and so strong that ten men couldn't lift his sword. When he came before the princess he bowed low and expressed his love for her, confident that she wouldn't refuse to be his wife.

But the princess didn't speak. The God of Autumn looked into her dark eyes and saw there was no spark of love there, despite his magnificent figure and noble birth. She shook her head.

The God of Autumn felt wounded to the heart. Fighting back bitter tears, he turned and walked away.

His younger brother, the God of Spring, who had accompanied him, was waiting outside in the palace garden.

"Did the princess agree to be your wife?" he asked.

"No!" snapped his brother. "She is too proud. She will never find a better husband than me."

The God of Spring smiled. "Then I'm going to ask her to marry me tomorrow," he said.

His brother stared at him in amazement.

"You!" The God of Autumn roared with laughter. "Why would the princess marry a boy like you when she wouldn't accept a man like me? You'll only make a fool of yourself."

"I don't care," sighed the God of Spring. "I saw her walking here in the palace garden and knew at once that I must ask her to be my wife."

"Then let's have a bet," said the God of Autumn. "If she says yes, I'll give you a cask of rice wine for your wedding. But if she says nothing, then you must give a cask to me."

The God of Spring accepted the bet. He went straight home to see his mother and told her about the princess. "Will you help me win her for my wife?" he asked.

His mother saw the true love in her son's heart. "You will need a new robe and sandals if you are going to the palace," she said, "and a fine bow and arrows. I will make them for you myself."

The God of Spring thanked his mother and that night, as he slept, she got to work.

First, she fetched a basket and went out into the garden. By the light of the moon, she filled the basket with curling tendrils from a wisteria tree and long sprays of flower buds. Then she magically wove the wisteria into a robe for her son. When it was done, she made him a pair of sandals from the twining stems and a bow and arrows.

In the morning, she gave them all to the God of Spring. He was disappointed to see how simple and dull the robe was, but he didn't want to be ungrateful, so he thanked her and put it on. Then he slipped his feet into the sandals and took up the bow and arrows.

"Wish me well, mother," he said and he set off for the palace.

When it was his turn to come before the princess, the God of Spring bowed humbly, his hopeful heart burning with love.

The princess's maids whispered to each other. "How could such a dull-looking boy, dressed in grey, marry the most beautiful princess, Dear Delight of the World?" they murmured.

But when the princess raised her eyes and gazed at the God of Spring, the wisteria buds woven into his robe burst into flower; purple and white blossom cascaded from his shoulders to his feet and the whole chamber was filled with its sweet scent.

The princess smiled. She rose and offered him her hand. "I will be your wife, my Lord, if you will have me," she said.

The God of Spring rushed to tell his brother the good news. "You owe me a cask of rice wine to drink at my wedding!" he said happily. But the God of Autumn scowled with jealousy. He refused to give his brother anything. "I wish you both nothing but misery," he thundered.

When the God of Spring brought the princess home to meet his mother, he told them both about his brother's anger.

"I'm sorry to hear it," said his mother, "but do not be afraid. All will be well for you."

With a heavy heart, she left them and went into the garden once more. There, she cut a hollow cane of bamboo and filled it with salt and stones. She wrapped the bamboo with leaves and hung it above the fire. With the fire-smoke curling around it, she spoke.

"As green leaves fade and die, so you must fade and die, my autumn son. As stone sinks in the sea, so you must sink. As the salt tide ebbs, so you too must ebb away."

And once her words were spoken, it was made to be. That is why spring will forever be fresh and merry and young, while autumn is the saddest time of year.

MAY

THE HARE IN THE MOON
A BUDDHIST STORY

Long ago, there was a wise and gentle hare, who lived in a wood at the foot of a mountain. Hare was kind and thoughtful. He always cared for everyone, even the tiniest beetle in the wood. The other animals loved to gather round to listen to his stories and learn his wise ways, especially his friends, Monkey, Jackal and Otter.

One night, as the four friends sat under the starry sky, Hare looked up and smiled. "We have learnt how to live happily together," he said, "but think how much more wonderful it would be if we could bring happiness to others."

"How can we do that?" asked Monkey.

Hare thought for a moment. "We should care for whoever comes to our wood by giving them what they need," he suggested.

"That's a good plan," said Jackal and the others agreed.

The next day, a poor man, dressed in rags, came to the wood. He was so thin that he was little more than skin and bone. Over his shoulder he carried a sack.

The man came to the riverbank where Otter lived and asked for food. Otter swam off and returned with a fish which he gave to the man, who put it in his sack.

Further down the track, the man met Jackal and once more asked for food. Jackal tramped off to a village nearby and returned with a pot of milk-curd. He gave it to the man, who put it in his sack.

Then Monkey scampered along. As before, the man asked for food, so Monkey climbed up a tree and picked a bunch of sweet mangoes. Into the sack they went.

MAY

Now Hare saw the hungry-looking man and thought, "Here is a chance to care for somebody's needs. I shall find food for him to eat."

Hare bounded off in search of something delicious, but all he could collect was grass. "Even a hungry man won't eat grass," he thought, sadly. "If only I could bring beans or rice." Then, as he thought about the things a man would eat, he suddenly realised that there was something he could offer.

Hare returned to the man, who was gathering sticks to make a fire, and watched as he unwrapped his bundle and pulled out a cooking pot, which he hung from a pole over the flames. Before long the pot was bubbling and the smell of fish cooking brought the other animals close.

Hare stepped forward. "I see you are hungry and need food," he said, "but I have no beans or rice to give you. Instead, I offer myself, for I know a man will eat a hare from the pot." And with these words he shook his fur to make sure there were no insects in his coat, then he sprung forward into the cooking pot.

At once, the pot and the fire disappeared.

To Hare's surprise, he landed, not in the boiling water, but in the arms of the man.

The other animals watched in astonishment.

"Gentle Hare," said the man, setting him down in the grass, "I am not a hungry stranger, I am the Lord of the Heaven above the Mountain. I heard about your generosity and came to see if what I heard was true."

"It is true," said Hare's friends. "Hare is the kindest creature in the wood."

Then the rags fell away and the Lord of the Heaven above the Mountain began to grow. He grew and grew before their eyes until he was big enough to put his arms around the mountain and squeeze it, so that the water in the rocks flowed out. Then he dipped his finger into the rock water, reached up into the sky and drew the figure of the hare onto the face of the moon.

"Now the world will remember the hare who wanted to bring happiness to others," said the Lord of the Heaven above the Mountain.

And if you look up at the moon on a dark night, you may see the hare for yourself.

JUNE

JUNE 8TH
WORLD OCEANS DAY

JUNE

PRINCE FIRE FLASH AND PRINCE FIRE FADE
A JAPANESE STORY

Prince Fire Flash was a fine fisherman. He caught things broad of fin and narrow of fin and knew the ways of the rivers and the sea.

His younger brother, Prince Fire Fade, was a skilled hunter. He caught things rough of hair and soft of hair and knew the ways of the woods and hills.

One day, Prince Fire Fade said to his brother, "Why don't we exchange tools and try each other's work? I will lend you my bow and borrow your fish hook."

At first, Prince Fire Flash was not too keen on this idea, but his brother kept asking until he agreed. So, next morning, they exchanged tools and wished each other good luck.

Prince Fire Flash didn't know the ways of the woods and hills and caught nothing all day. His brother had no success either and, what was worse, he lost the fish hook in the sea.

When Prince Fire Flash heard that his fish hook had been lost he was very angry.

Prince Fire Fade took his long sword, broke it into pieces and made five hundred fish hooks. "Take these in exchange for the one I lost," he said. But Prince Fire Flash refused to accept them.

Then Prince Fire Fade made five hundred more and offered them to his brother. "Here are a thousand fish hooks to replace one."

But Prince Fire Flash was still angry. "I won't have any except my own!" he said.

Prince Fire Fade sat by the shore and cried bitterly. Along came the Wise Old Man of the Sea and asked why he was so unhappy. Prince Fire Fade told him the story of the lost fish hook.

"It's my own fault," he cried, "but I don't know how to make things right."

The Wise Old Man of the Sea made a little boat out of plaited bamboo leaves. "Sail out to sea until this boat begins to sink," he said. "Deep down beneath the waves you will find the palace of the Sea King, and there you will meet the Sea King's daughter, who will tell you what to do."

Prince Fire Fade did as he was told, and when the little boat sank beneath the waves he came to a palace shimmering with fishes' scales. In front of the palace, beside a well, was a cassia tree. Prince Fire Fade climbed out of the boat and hid himself in the tree.

Before long, Princess Pearl, the Sea King's daughter, came to sit by the well. At once, Prince Fire Fade was fascinated by her strange watery beauty. When she saw his reflection in the well she gasped, and rushed away to tell her father that there was a handsome stranger in the tree.

"This is Prince Fire Fade, the great hunter!" said the Sea King and he welcomed him with a fine banquet.

Prince Fire Fade stayed and spent many days, walking with the princess among the shifting green shadows and coral gardens of the palace, quite forgetting why he had come there. Soon they fell in love and were married, and for three years they lived happily together in their undersea home.

Then, one day, Princess Pearl noticed a faraway look in her husband's eyes. He told her how he had lost his brother's fish hook and wished he could return it.

"I shall help you," said the princess. She went to the steps of the palace and summoned all the creatures of the sea, great and small. From the sunlit shallows and the darkest depths they came, and the water flashed silver with a thousand fins and scales.

"My husband wishes to find the fish hook of Prince Fire Flash," she explained.

A lobster spoke up. "The Tai has been complaining of something stuck in his throat," he said, "but I don't see him here." So, a messenger was sent to fetch the Tai, who did indeed have a fish hook caught in his throat and was feeling very sorry for himself.

"Let me remove it for you," said Princess Pearl. She took the Tai gently in her hands and, with her delicate fingers, released the fish hook.

"That is the one!" cried Prince Fire Fade joyfully. "Now I must return it to my brother."

Before Prince Fire Fade left, the Sea King gave him two jewels. "This one rules the flow of the tide," he explained, "and this one rules the ebb. If your brother is still angry with you, bring out the tide-flowing jewel and he will be drowned. If he asks your forgiveness, bring out the tide-ebbing jewel and he will be saved." Then the king called up a great sea-dragon to carry Prince Fire Fade home.

When Prince Fire Fade reached the shore he saw his brother nearby and hurried to return the fish hook. But Prince Fire Flash was still angry with him. So Prince Fire Fade brought out the tide-flowing jewel and at once his brother found the sea rising in a great turmoil around him.

"Save me, brother!" cried Prince Fire Flash, afraid he would drown. "I was wrong not to forgive you."

Prince Fire Fade brought out the tide-ebbing jewel and the sea subsided. At last the two brothers were happily reunited.

Then Prince Fire Fade built a house, thatched with cormorant feathers, and Princess Pearl came to him, bringing the happy news that she would soon bear him a child.

JUNE

JUNE
RAMADAN

THE BOOTS OF HUNAIN
AN ARABIC STORY

One morning, a desert traveller rode into town and noticed a pair of boots outside a cobbler's shop. He went inside and offered some money to buy them.

"Those are the finest boots I've ever made," said Hunain, the cobbler. "They're worth three times that amount."

"That's far too much!" scoffed the traveller. He tried to persuade Hunain to lower the price. But no matter how much they argued, Hunain wouldn't part with the wonderful boots for less.

The traveller grew angry. "You are a stubborn, greedy man," he said. "My camel is worth that price!" And he stormed out of the shop.

Hunain felt insulted by the traveller's rude words. Moments later, when he saw the traveller ride past on his camel, Hunain grabbed the boots and followed. He watched which route the traveller took into the desert and hurried along a shortcut to get ahead of him.

A mile along the trail, Hunain placed one boot in the sand and a mile further, he placed the second boot. Then he hid behind a sand dune.

The traveller rode along, grumbling to himself about the cobbler, until he saw the first boot lying in the sand.

"That's the very boot I wanted!" he exclaimed. "But sadly one is no use." So he rode on.

Soon, he found the second boot. "What luck!" he laughed. "I'll go back for the other one, then I'll have a pair for nothing!"

The traveller didn't want to tire out his camel, so he tied her up and hurried off on foot.

As soon as he was out of sight, Hunain untied the camel.

"Fair's fair," he chuckled, and he climbed onto the camel's back and rode home.

JUNE
MIDSUMMER

ANANSI AND TURTLE
A CARIBBEAN STORY

One hot summer's day, Turtle went for a walk. After a while, he began to feel hungry. He smelt something cooking nearby and followed the delicious smell until he came to the house of Anansi the Spider Man.

Anansi was sitting in the sun outside his house, just about to eat his lunch. On the table before him was a big bowl of sweet roasted yams.

"Hello, Anansi," said Turtle. "I'm very hungry, can I share your lunch?"

"No!" said Anansi. "I've grown these yams and roasted them and I'm going to eat every one myself."

Turtle gazed at the yams and felt hungrier than ever. "That's not kind," he said. "It's good manners to offer food to anyone who comes to your home."

Anansi frowned. "Well, all right then," he agreed. So Turtle sat down at the table. However, as soon as he reached out for a yam, Anansi jumped up.

"Look at your hands, Turtle," he said. "You can't come to the table with dirty hands! Go down to the river and wash them."

Turtle couldn't deny that his hands were dirty, so he went to wash them in the river. While he was gone, Anansi quickly ate as many yams as he could.

When Turtle returned, he was hungrier than ever. But Anansi still wouldn't let him eat.

"Look at your hands, Turtle," he said, "you've made them dirty again walking back from the river! You should have walked on the grass. You can't sit at the table with dirty hands."

So Turtle went back to the river. While he was gone, Anansi quickly ate up the rest of the yams.

When Turtle returned and found the bowl empty, Anansi just smiled. "I hope you've enjoyed your lunch, Turtle," he said. "Now I have things to do."

Turtle nodded thoughtfully. "First, you must agree to come to lunch at my house, Anansi," he said. "You must let me return the favour."

Anansi always liked to get something for nothing, so he agreed to visit Turtle the following day.

The next day, Anansi walked down to the creek where Turtle lived. "Turtle looks very well fed," he thought to himself, "I expect I'm in for a big feast!"

When he arrived Turtle greeted him. "The table is laid, Anansi," he said. "Please follow me," and he dived down to the bottom of the creek.

Anansi jumped into the water and followed. Down he went, deeper and deeper, until he saw a table full of delicious looking food. "Take a seat, Anansi," said Turtle.

Anansi licked his greedy lips, but as soon as he sat down… whoop… he felt himself shooting up to the surface again! He wasn't heavy enough to stay at the bottom of the creek!

"Hmm!" Anansi was determined to eat Turtle's lunch. He searched for some stones on the river bank and put them in his jacket pockets, then he jumped into the water once more. This time, he sank down and stayed down. But as he reached out for something to eat, Turtle shook his head.

"Oh no, Anansi," said Turtle. "It's not polite to wear your jacket at the table. You must remove it."

So Anansi took off his jacket and… whoop… he shot up to the surface again!

Anansi climbed onto the riverbank, coughing and spluttering. As he shook himself dry, Turtle peeped out of the water.

"I hope you enjoyed your lunch, Anansi," he said. "It was so good that there's nothing left!"

JUNE

JUNE 21ST
WORLD MUSIC DAY

SKELETON WOMAN
AN INUIT STORY

JUNE

Once there was a lonely hunter who had caught nothing for many days. He paddled his kayak from cove to cove, looking for fish without any luck, until he came to a tiny, deserted bay.

"Maybe my luck will change here," he thought, so he went ashore and built himself a snow house. When it was finished, the hunter paddled out to the middle of the bay and lowered his fishing hook deep into the water.

All afternoon he caught nothing. As the sun began to set, he feared he would spend another hungry night without supper. But just when he was about to give up, the fishing line jerked.

"At last!" cried the hunter, gripping his rod. "This feels like a huge fish. It will feed me for a week!"

With a mighty heave, he pulled the catch out of the water. To his horror, it was not a fish on the end of the line – it was a skeleton, draped in weed, with sea-worms writhing from its eye sockets and crabs clinging to its ribs!

The hunter screamed in terror and dropped the rod. Shaking with fear, he scrambled for the paddle and rowed towards the shore as fast as his arms could pull him through the water.

But the skeleton was still hooked to the line. It clattered behind the kayak with its arms flying and legs rattling as if it was running over the waves.

When he reached the shore, the hunter leapt out of the kayak, grabbed his rod and ran towards the snow house, too frightened to look behind. The skeleton followed, rolling its gruesome skull from side to side and snatching at the air with bony fingers.

Panting for breath, the hunter reached the snow house, dived into the entrance

tunnel and crawled inside. "Safe at last!" he gasped.

He crouched on his bed in the darkness, still trembling with fear at what he'd seen. Taking a deep breath, he calmed himself and thanked the spirits for his narrow escape. But when he lit his oil lamp, the hunter saw he was not alone... the skeleton lay in a jumbled heap of bones on the floor!

The hunter froze...

The skeleton didn't stir. Its bones lay tangled up in the fishing line, a knee inside the ribcage, a foot over the shoulder and the arms cradling the skull.

For a while, the hunter was too afraid to move, but as he gazed at the still, solemn face in the lamplight, a deep sadness came over him. He crept close and touched the skeleton's hand. He gently lifted the skull and stroked its cold head. Before he realised what he was doing, the hunter began to draw out the fishing line and untangle the bones, laying them out, one by one, as a body should peacefully lay. While he worked, he sang a soft, mournful song.

When he had finished, the hunter saw that the skeleton was a woman. He covered her in warm seal skins. "Who was she?" he

JUNE

wondered. "Why did she lie at the bottom of the bay?" Feeling tired from his ordeal, he climbed into bed and was soon asleep.

As the hunter slept, he dreamed, and a tear ran down his cheek.

Slowly, the skeleton woman turned her head. She pushed back the covers and crept over to the hunter. Bringing her face close to his, she caught the salty tear in her mouth. Then she slipped a hand inside his chest and pulled out his heart.

The skeleton woman beat the hunter's heart like a drum – she played the rhythm of life and she began to sing. She sang for her flesh to return; for her eyes, to see the sun rise; for her feet, to dance; her hands, to sew fine boots; for her belly, to grow a child; for her own heart, to love. All night the skeleton woman drummed and sang the song of life and when the song had made her whole, she slipped the hunter's heart back inside his chest.

When the hunter woke next morning, he saw the beautiful woman lying beside him. "My luck has truly changed!" he marvelled and he thanked the spirits, for he knew he would never be hungry or lonely again.

JULY

ZIRAK AND RING-DOVE
AN IRAQI STORY

Ring-dove and her sisters found a scatter of safflower seeds one morning. They started pecking, so happy to have a delicious breakfast that they didn't notice a net in the grass beneath their feet.

Suddenly, the net closed around them and they were trapped!

Ring-dove's sisters flapped and fluttered in a panic.

"Stay calm," said Ring-dove, "I see the bird-catcher coming. If we each struggle to save ourselves we shall all be caught. We must work together to escape."

"But what can we do?" cried her sisters desperately.

"Let's try flapping our wings together," said Ring-dove. "Maybe we can lift the net off the ground and fly out of the bird-catcher's reach." So, when Ring-dove cried "Fly!" everyone flapped together.

Just as the bird-catcher stretched out to grab the net, Ring-dove and her sisters rose from the ground like one huge bird and flew over his head and away.

"You won't escape from me!" shouted the bird-catcher, shaking his fist angrily. "That's my best net!" And he ran after them.

Ring-dove and her sisters flew as fast as they could, but the net was heavy and their wings soon grew tired. "We're still trapped," the sisters sighed, "and he'll catch us if we stop to rest!"

Ring-dove noticed they were near the town. "Let's fly there," she said. "The bird-catcher won't be able to follow us through the narrow, winding streets and I have a plan to set us free."

With all the strength they could muster, Ring-dove and her sisters flew on together, over the town wall, to a quiet alley, where they fluttered down and lay, exhausted, in the net.

As Ring-dove had guessed, the bird-catcher followed them into the town, but he was soon lost in the maze of streets and busy markets. When he realised that he'd never find the birds or the net, he gave up at last and went home.

Meanwhile, Ring-dove's sisters felt sorry for themselves. "We may have escaped the bird-catcher," they moaned, "but we're no safer here, in this town full of hungry cats and dogs."

"Trust me," said Ring-dove, "I told you I had a plan." She edged towards a little hole in the shadow of the street and called out.

"Zirak, friend Zirak!"

A brown mouse peered out of the hole. "Who calls my name?" he said, blinking at the sunlight.

"My sisters and I need your help," said Ring-dove.

Zirak ran to her side. "Ring-dove, old friend!" he cried. "How did you come to be tangled in this net?" Then Ring-dove explained how they had escaped from the bird-catcher.

At once, Zirak set about chewing the net to free his friend.

The sisters flapped and fretted. "Bite here!" they urged him. "Get me out first!" But Zirak ignored them and continued to make a hole for Ring-dove.

"Save my sisters first, Zirak," whispered Ring-dove. "Leave me until last."

"But they are selfish," exclaimed Zirak. "They don't care about each other."

"If you save me first, you may grow tired and leave them behind," said Ring-dove. "But I'm sure that if you leave me until last, you won't abandon your friend?"

Zirak chuckled to himself. "You're right, dear Ring-dove," he said. "I don't care about the fate of your silly sisters, but your kindness to them makes me love you even more."

So he chewed the net until he had freed the sisters and, at last, Ring-dove herself. And there was just time for the two friends to say goodbye, before a cat scampered up the alley and sent them all hurrying home.

JULY

JULY 7TH
TANABATA

THE WEAVING MAIDEN AND THE OXHERD

A JAPANESE STORY

JULY

On the banks of the Silver River of Heaven, lived a beautiful maiden called Orihime, the daughter of the Sky God. All day, she sat at her loom, weaving colourful silken threads to make splendid clothes for her father. Orihime's skill was admired by all the gods and she was known as the Weaving Maiden.

However, Orihime worked so hard that she forgot to spend time with the other maidens or look for a husband. Her father grew worried about her, but he could not persuade Orihime to leave the loom and enjoy the pleasures of life.

One day, he gently took the shuttle from her hand and covered the loom with a cloth. "As you will not look at anything but your threads," he said, "I have found a husband for you, Orihime." He brought before her the oxherd, Hikoboshi, who tended his beasts along the banks of the Silver River.

When Orihime saw the young oxherd, stars sparkled in her eyes. She rose from her loom and walked beside him along the riverbank and they talked of many things. Before long, they were married, with her father's blessing, and he was pleased to see his daughter's happiness.

However, once Orihime was married, she began to change. She no longer wanted to sit at her loom, but ran along the river bank, singing and dancing and laughing with Hikoboshi, while his oxen wandered, untended through the heavenly meadows.

The Sky God waited for his daughter to return to her duties, but she no longer cared for her shuttle and thread. "I'm enjoying the pleasures of life now, Father," she said happily, "just as you wanted me to."

The Sky God grew angry. "Who will weave my spring kimono?" he demanded. Three times he asked Orihime to return to her loom, but she just smiled and played with Hikoboshi among the blossom trees of heaven.

At last the Sky God lost his patience. He banished Hikoboshi the oxherd to the other side of the Silver River.

Then Orihime cried out across the river to her husband and wept at being parted from him, but no matter how much she pleaded with the Sky God, he would not relent.

Eventually, when all her tears were shed, Orihime returned to the loom and took up her shuttle and thread. Once more, she made fine garments for the Sky God, but gone were the colourful silks. Everything she made was drab and grey.

When he saw his daughter's sad face, the Sky God took pity on her.

"As you have returned to your weaving, Orihime," he said, "on the seventh day of the seventh month, I shall summon all the magpies from the ends of the earth to build a bridge across the Silver River."

And so it was. With hope in her heart, Orihime took up her colourful threads again, and when the seventh day of the seventh month dawned, all the magpies from the ends of the earth flew up to heaven and fluttered over the Silver River, spreading their wings to make a living bridge for the Weaving Maiden to cross, so that she could visit her husband, Hikoboshi, the oxherd.

Every year, on that night, Orihime's eyes sparkle brightly in the sky as she laughs once more with Hikoboshi, on the banks of the Silver River. But if rain falls, the magpies cannot spread their wings to make a bridge and the Weaving Maiden must wait another year to cross.

JULY

JULY 15TH
ST SWITHIN'S DAY

ELEPHANT AND THE RAIN SPIRIT
AN AFRICAN BUSHMAN STORY

Elephant was very proud of being the largest, strongest animal.
"I am the greatest in the land!" he boasted and nobody ever dared to argue with him.
One day, the Rain Spirit heard Elephant's words. "How can you be greater than me?" he asked.

Elephant raised his head. "Look at my mighty trunk and fine tusks," he cried. "See how the earth shakes when I stamp my feet. It's obvious that I'm the greatest in the land."

"But I fill the lakes, so that all animals can drink," said the Rain Spirit. "I water the plants for them to eat. Surely I'm more powerful than you?"

Nobody had ever challenged Elephant before. He flapped his ears in annoyance. "I don't need anyone to find me food and drink," he roared. "I can take care of myself."

Then the sky grew dark and cracked with thunder. "So be it," said the Rain Spirit. "I'll leave you to your own fate!" And with a flash of lightning, he disappeared.

Elephant swished his tail and laughed. "Old Rain Spirit has run away," he said. "I must be the greatest in the land!"

After that, Elephant swaggered about, feeling more pleased with himself than before.

However, when the rainy season arrived, there was no rain to fill the lakes and water the plants. The animals grew hungry and thirsty. They came to see Elephant.

"You are the greatest among us," they said. "Give us water to drink. Make rain fall on the plants so we can have food to eat."

Elephant shuffled his huge feet in the dust and frowned. "Ask Crow to make rain," he said.

Crow flew into the sky and did her best, but she could only produce enough rain to fill a few waterholes. The animals soon drank them dry, all except one, which Elephant claimed for himself.

"This is my waterhole," he announced loudly and he commanded Tortoise to watch over it.

The next day, while Elephant was looking for food, the other animals crept up to the waterhole.

"You can't drink here," said Tortoise. "This is Elephant's water."

"But we're so thirsty," sighed the springbok.

"We won't drink it all," promised the giraffes.

"Let us just take a sip," pleaded the zebras.

"No. Not a drop," said Tortoise firmly.

Then along came Lion.

"You can't drink here," said Tortoise, but Lion took no notice. He swept Tortoise away with his paw and sent him tumbling across the sand. Then Lion took a drink and the others followed, slurping and lapping until all the water was gone.

When Elephant returned, feeling very thirsty, he saw the empty waterhole and flew into a terrible rage. "Who dared to drink my water?" he roared.

"I tried to stop them!" cried Tortoise. But Elephant was so angry that he picked Tortoise up with his trunk and swallowed him whole.

"It's all your fault!" shouted Tortoise, inside Elephant's stomach. He began to stamp and butt Elephant with his hard head.

"Stamp, stamp, stamp," went Tortoise.

"Ouch!" cried Elephant, rubbing his belly.

"Butt, butt, butt," went Tortoise.

"Stop!" bellowed Elephant, sinking to his knees.

Suddenly the sky grew dark. "What's all this noise?" said the Rain Spirit.

"Help!" cried Elephant.

"Help you, the greatest in the land?" said the Rain Spirit.

"I'm not the greatest in the sky," whimpered Elephant.

Then the Rain Spirit burst out laughing and his laughter rained down and filled the lakes and watered all the plants.

And when he heard the rain, Tortoise gave Elephant such a fierce butt with his head that Elephant coughed him out again.

JULY

JULY 30TH
INTERNATIONAL DAY OF FRIENDSHIP

HEUNGBU AND NOLBU
A KOREAN STORY

Once there were two brothers, Nolbu and Heungbu, who lived together with their families in their father's house. Nolbu, the eldest, was selfish and cruel, but his brother, Heungbu, was always kind.

When their father died, Nolbu threw Heungbu out of the house and kept all of their father's fortune for himself. Heungbu had to live in a tumbledown hovel and work hard to feed his family, but he never complained.

One autumn, the harvest was bad and Heungbu's family had nothing to eat, so he went to his brother's house to beg for some food for his children. Nolbu's wife, who was just as cruel as her husband, was cooking in the kitchen.

When she saw Heungbu, she refused to give him anything and struck him on the face with her rice ladle. But Heungbu didn't complain. Carefully, he scraped the sticky rice from his cheek and asked her to strike him again. Thinking him stupid, she did as he asked. Then Heungbu gathered the rice from the other cheek and took it home to feed his children.

The next day, Heungbu found a young swallow that had fallen from its nest. Gently, he bandaged its broken leg, then he cared for it until it was strong enough to return to the nest.

That winter, the swallow flew away, but it didn't forget Heungbu's kindness. When it returned in the spring, the swallow dropped some seeds into his hand. Heungbu had no garden, so he planted them on his thatched roof.

Before long, vines began to grow on the roof. They produced bright flowers and then three plump gourds.

When the gourds were ripe, Heungbu borrowed a ladder and picked them.

"These will feed us all for weeks," he said and he cut one open. To the family's amazement, the gourd was full of rice, which flowed and flowed until it had filled a dozen sacks.

"Open another!" said his wife. Out of the second gourd tumbled enough gold coins to fill a cart.

"Open another!" cried the children. Out of the third gourd, Heungbu pulled enough timber and nails to build a fine house.

Laughing with happiness, Heungbu and his family set to work to build themselves a house, and when it was built they shared their good fortune with their neighbours.

The story of Heungbu's good luck soon reached his brother's ears. Nolbu went at once to see how such a thing could have happened. He listened in amazement, as Heungbu told him about the swallow and the gourd seeds.

Immediately, Nolbu was jealous of his brother's good fortune. He returned home and searched for a swallow's nest. When he found one, he snatched up a young bird and broke its leg. Then he bandaged it roughly and flung it back in the nest.

As before, the swallow flew south for the winter. When it returned in the spring, the swallow dropped some seeds into Nolbu's hand and he planted them in his garden.

Nolbu and his wife waited impatiently for their gourds to grow. As soon as they were ripe, Nolbu fetched his saw to cut them open.

"Now we'll be even richer!" they cried greedily. But to their horror, out of the gourds leapt a dozen wicked goblins, shrieking wildly. The goblins stole Nolbu's money and tore down his house.

Nolbu and his wife were left with nothing. In tears, they went to Heungbu and humbly asked for help.

Heungbu welcomed them. "My house is your house, brother," he said. And so Nolbu and his wife learnt kindness, and they all lived happily ever after.

JULY

ANDROCLES AND THE LION
A ROMAN STORY

JULY

Androcles was a Roman slave who belonged to a harsh master. Although he worked hard, he was left to sleep on the ground and eat from the dog's bowl. One night, after a cruel beating, Androcles decided he could bear no more.

When his master was asleep, Androcles climbed out of the window and fled. He didn't stop running until he reached the mountains. Exhausted and hungry, he found shelter in a cave and lay down to rest.

Suddenly, he heard a terrifying growl and a lion appeared at the cave entrance. Androcles shrank back in horror. To his astonishment, the lion didn't leap to devour him, but limped forward with a swollen paw. It lay down and groaned deeply. Androcles crept close and saw a thorn embedded in its pad. Although he was afraid, he couldn't bear to see any creature suffer. With trembling fingers, he carefully removed the thorn. Then he tore a strip of cloth from his tunic to clean the wound and bandaged the paw. The lion raised his shaggy head and licked Androcles's hand gratefully.

Androcles stayed with the lion for several days, until he was healed, then he said goodbye and set off down the mountain.

However, that morning, the master's men were riding by. "Here's the runaway slave!" they cried and they took Androcles off to prison.

"What will happen to me?" Androcles asked.

"Runaways are thrown to the beasts, in the emperor's arena," grunted the guard. "We starve them first, so they'll be hungry!"

A week later, Androcles was taken to the arena. As he walked out before the emperor, the huge crowd jeered. There was nowhere to run and nowhere to hide. Androcles shut his eyes tight.

He heard a ferocious roar and the crowd cheered. Androcles shuddered as he waited for the teeth and jaws of a beast — but two paws landed on his shoulders and a warm tongue licked his face!

He opened his eyes. There, before him was the lion.

"Old friend!" Androcles laughed. "So they captured you too!" The crowd fell silent in amazement.

"Bring the boy to me," said the emperor.

When he heard the slave boy's story, the emperor smiled. "You have earned your freedom by your kindness, Androcles," he said. "Now take your friend back to the mountain, where he belongs."

AUGUST

AUGUST 1ST
LAMMAS DAY

THE LITTLE RED HEN
A RUSSIAN STORY

AUGUST

Little Red Hen lived in the farmyard with her six lively chicks, who kept her busy all day, feeding them and keeping them out of mischief. One morning, she was scratching for worms when she found some grains of wheat.

"You could plant that wheat," said the pig, lying lazily in his sty.

"Then you could make flour," said the cat, basking in the sun.

"And use it to bake delicious bread," said the duck, paddling idly in the pond.

"What a good idea," said Little Red Hen and she gathered up the wheat. "Who will help me plant it?" she asked.

"Not I," said the pig.

"Not I," said the cat.

"Not I," said the duck. So Little Red Hen planted the wheat herself.

All summer the wheat grew and the chicks grew too. They were hungry from the moment they woke up until they fell asleep. Little Red Hen had no rest at all.

"Who will help me cut the wheat?" she asked.

"Not I," said the pig.

"Not I," said the cat.

"Not I," said the duck.

"Well, I'll just have to do it myself," sighed Little Red Hen and she cut the wheat, while the chicks played excitedly in the straw.

But the wheat couldn't be made into flour until it was threshed.

Little Red Hen put her giddy chicks to bed and then she asked "Who will help me thresh this wheat?"

"Not I," said the pig.

"Not I," said the cat.

"Not I," said the duck.

"It seems I must do it myself," said Little Red Hen with a yawn, and she threshed the wheat alone.

Next morning, Little Red Hen put the wheat into a sack to take to the mill. The chicks tried to climb in too, but she made them walk behind as she set off up the hill.

On the way home, the chicks raced down the hill and tumbled into a muddy pond at the bottom.

"Tomorrow, you stay behind!" said Little Red Hen when she'd cleaned them all up.

The following day, Little Red Hen was eager to collect her flour. "Who will help me carry my flour from the mill?" she asked.

"Not I," said the pig.

"Not I," said the cat.

"Not I," said the duck.

"Well, a walk will give me a good appetite," snapped Little Red Hen and she went to collect her flour.

When she returned, the chicks pecked the sack and covered themselves in flour.

"Shoo, shoo, shoo!" cried Little Red Hen, chasing them away. "Out to play, and don't get into trouble!"

"Now, who will help me make the bread?" she asked.

"Not I," said the pig.

"Not I," said the cat.

"Not I," said the duck.

"Hmmm!" Little Red Hen frowned and put on her apron. Then she mixed the flour into a dough, let it rise, and made three fine loaves for the oven.

When the loaves were cooked, a delicious smell wafted out of Little Red Hen's kitchen. The hungry chicks came running… and so did the pig, the cat and the duck.

"Let us help you eat that bread," said the pig, the cat and the duck. But Little Red Hen shook her head.

"I planted this wheat," she said. "I cut it and threshed it, I carried it to the mill and brought back the flour and I baked this beautiful bread. Now, my hungry chicks and I are going to eat it – so, shoo, shoo, shoo!"

And Little Red Hen chased the pig, the cat and the duck right out of her house!

AUGUST

AUGUST
HARVEST

THE SHIP OF WHEAT
A DUTCH STORY

AUGUST

Long ago, on the shores of the Zuyder Zee, stood a wealthy city called Stavoren. Stavoren had a fine harbour that was always bustling with ships, carrying cargo from distant lands. Its merchants became so rich that they ate from silver dishes.

The wealthiest of these merchants was a proud lady, who lived in a grand house. The lady of Stavoren wore rubies and pearls and slept on a golden bed, carved with peacocks, but she was never happy. She always wanted something more, to show that she was richer than everyone else.

One day, the lady of Stavoren called for the captain of her fleet and asked him to find her the most precious thing in the world.

The captain set sail, wondering what would please her. For three months he searched for something special, but nothing he found seemed precious enough. He asked the crew for help.

"Well, there's one precious thing we can't live without, Captain," said the crew, "and that's bread, to fill our stomachs!"

"Of course!" said the captain. "Nobody, rich or poor, can live without bread. It must be the most precious thing." So he bought a hundred sacks of fine, golden wheat and set sail for home.

Meanwhile, the lady of Stavoren had been boasting to her friends that she would soon own the most precious thing in the world. The moment the captain's ship appeared in the harbour, she went down to the quay and everyone followed to see what he'd brought her.

When the lady was shown a hundred sacks of wheat, she flew into a rage!

"How dare you waste my money on a ship full of wheat!" she cried.

"But it's the most precious thing in the world," protested the captain. "No-one can live without it."

"Well I can live without it!" she cried. "Throw it all overboard!"

At these words, a young boy pushed his way through the crowd.

"Let me have some, lady," he begged. "My mother has nothing to feed us." The lady of Stavoren glared at him, her eyes blazing with anger. "It's mine!" she said. "Nobody else shall have it!"

With heavy hearts, the crew started to heave the sacks of wheat over the side of the ship.

"You might be begging for bread yourself one day," muttered the captain, "and then you'll regret this."

The lady took a ring from her finger and dropped it into the harbour. "That ring will return to me before I ever beg for anything," she snapped and she walked off.

At supper, the following evening, the lady was served a fish. When she cut it open, there, to her astonishment, was her ring. She turned pale. Before she could push the dish away, a messenger arrived and reported that all her ships had been wrecked in a storm.

That night, lightning set fire to her house; everything she owned was destroyed and she barely escaped with her life.

None of the lady's rich friends would help her, seeing she was poor, and in a sudden change of fortune she found herself begging for bread on the street.

Meanwhile, at the bottom of the harbour, the wheat grains took root. They grew up through the water, trapping sand between their stems, until a great sandbar blocked the harbour, preventing ships from passing in or out. In a short time, all the rich merchants of Stavoren were ruined and they too found themselves begging for bread.

Out in the harbour, the lady's wheat grew tall and straight, but it was barren and didn't offer them one single grain.

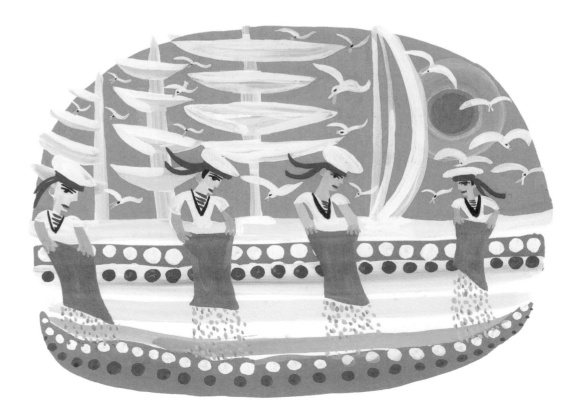

AUGUST

AUGUST
HARVEST

PERSEPHONE

AN ANCIENT GREEK STORY

Mighty Zeus was the King of the Gods. He lived at the top of a mountain called Olympus, where he watched over all the gods and goddesses and the lives of the people below.

His brother, Hades, was the King of the Underworld, god of the deep, dark earth and everything in it.

Zeus and Hades had a sister named Demeter, who walked the surface of the earth giving life to plants and trees. She was the Goddess of the Harvest, producing fruit and vegetables and grain to feed the people of the world.

One day, Hades felt lonely, living by himself in his silent kingdom. He went to ask his brother, Zeus, how to find a wife.

"Demeter has a beautiful daughter, called Persephone," said Zeus. "She would brighten your dark days, but you'll have to steal her away from her mother."

Hades secretly watched Persephone and fell in love with her sparkling eyes and cheerful laughter. But he also saw that she was happiest dancing through the meadows with Demeter.

So, he waited until she was picking flowers alone one morning and commanded the earth to split open in a great chasm. Then he leapt into his chariot and up, out of the chasm he rode. Before Persephone realised what was happening, Hades swept her into his arms and carried her back down to the Underworld. At once, the chasm closed behind them and all that was left were Persephone's flowers, lying in the grass.

Demeter searched for her daughter, calling her name over and over, but she was nowhere to be found. Days passed and Persephone didn't return. Demeter grew desperately sad. Nothing thrived, nothing blossomed or bore fruit while she wandered the world, looking for her beloved daughter.

Meanwhile, down in the Underworld, Hades tried to win Persephone's heart. He decorated a chamber with glistening

gemstones, collected from the rocks of the earth, and gold and silver, mined beneath the mountains, but she only wanted to return to her mother above.

Demeter lost all joy without Persephone. Plants withered, crops failed and the earth became barren.

Zeus saw that the people of the world were hungry and feared they would soon be blaming him for their fate. He sent his messenger, Hermes, to visit Hades and ask him to let Persephone return to her mother.

Hades did not dare to disobey his powerful brother, Zeus. But before he let Persephone leave, he offered her a token of his love – a scarlet pomegranate. Persephone suddenly felt sorry for Hades, living alone in his sunless kingdom. "After all," she thought, "it cannot be wrong to wish for happiness." Before Hermes could stop her, she ate four pomegranate seeds.

Then Hades smiled. "Now we shall be together forever, Persephone!" he said.

To her dismay, Hermes explained that anyone who eats in the Underworld must return there.

When Persephone was reunited with her mother there was much joy and celebration, but it was tinged with sadness at the news of the pomegranate seeds.

Demeter went to plead with Zeus. "Don't send my daughter away forever," she cried.

Zeus frowned thoughtfully. He took pity on his sister. "For each seed that Persephone ate in the Underworld, she shall spend one month with Hades, who loves her dearly," he said. "But for the rest of the year she shall return to you."

And so it was and has been ever since. Each year, in the spring and summer months, Demeter and Persephone dance and laugh together, bringing life and growth to the world; wherever they pass, plants burst into leaf, flowers blossom, fruit ripens and grain swells to fill the granaries.

But in the autumn, Persephone returns to Hades, in the Underworld, and Demeter mourns for her daughter. Then the leaves fall, plants die and the winter earth lies cold and bare.

AUGUST

SEPTEMBER

SEPTEMBER
YOM KIPPUR

JONAH AND THE WHALE
A BIBLE STORY

God was unhappy with the people of the city of Nineveh, because they'd forgotten how to live good lives and had learnt wicked ways.

He asked Jonah to travel to Nineveh. "Tell the people they must change their ways," said God, "and ask forgiveness for the bad things they've done."

Jonah agreed to do what God asked. But he didn't think the wicked people of Nineveh should be forgiven, he thought it was right that they should be punished.

Instead of going to Nineveh, Jonah boarded a boat sailing far away to Tarshish, in the opposite direction. Knowing that he was disobeying God, Jonah hid himself below the deck.

However, soon after the voyage began, dark clouds gathered and a great storm tossed the boat violently on the water. The sailors had never seen such fierce wind and rain and they were afraid the boat would sink.

"What has caused this sudden tempest?" they cried.

Jonah was woken from his sleep. He made his way onto the deck. "I'm sure this storm is a punishment because I disobeyed God," he said. "If you throw me overboard the sea will be calm and you'll be safe."

The sailors didn't want to throw anyone overboard. They tried with all their might to row to shore but it was impossible to struggle against the waves. At last, terrified that they'd all lose their lives, they did as Jonah said.

The moment Jonah was thrown overboard the storm stopped and the sea became calm again. But God didn't let Jonah drown, he sent a huge whale to swallow him whole.

Inside the dark belly of the whale, Jonah thanked God for saving him and said he was sorry for running away from the task he'd been given. After three days and nights inside the whale, God commanded the gentle creature to spit Jonah out on the shore.

Once more, God asked Jonah to go to Nineveh. "Warn the people that they have forty days to change their wicked ways and show they are sorry," he said, "or I shall destroy their city."

This time, Jonah went straight to Nineveh. He walked through the streets, giving the people God's message. To his surprise, they listened and his warning quickly spread throughout the city. People realised they must stop behaving badly and were sorry for the wicked things they'd done. When the king heard Jonah's words, he too humbly begged for God's forgiveness.

Then Jonah went outside the city walls and made himself a shelter. There he waited and watched to see if Nineveh would be destroyed.

Day after day, under the hot sun, Jonah watched and waited. God made a leafy vine to grow over the shelter and give him shade, then he sent a worm to eat the roots and the vine withered and died.

Jonah gazed sadly at the vine and God spoke to him.

"Jonah, you feel sorry for the vine, although you didn't plant it or make it grow," he said. "Shouldn't I have pity for all the people in the great city of Nineveh?"

Then Jonah was ashamed of his unforgiving heart. He understood how much God loved his people and wanted them to love him too. And so the city of Nineveh was saved.

SEPTEMBER

SEPTEMBER 21ST
INTERNATIONAL DAY OF PEACE

THE TWO KINGS
A BUDDHIST STORY

Brahmadatta was the king of Benares and famous for his wise judgement. His neighbour, King Mallika, also believed that he treated his people fairly.

One day, King Brahmadatta decided to disguise himself as a merchant and travel around the land to see if there were any complaints in his kingdom. He didn't know that King Mallika had decided to do the very same thing.

The two kings disguised themselves and rode around the countryside in their chariots.

They travelled for many days, without hearing any complaints from their people, until they both came to the edge of their kingdoms and met at the same spot. As there was no room to pass on the narrow road, the chariots halted.

"Move out of the way!" shouted one of the drivers. "This is the great King Mallika."

"No, you move!" cried the second driver. "I'm carrying the great King Brahmadatta."

The two chariot drivers climbed down and eyed each other, thoughtfully. "If our masters are equally great, how can we decide who must make way?" they wondered.

"The youngest should make way for the oldest," suggested one of the drivers. But both kings were the same age.

"The smallest kingdom should give way to the largest," suggested the other driver. But both were exactly the same size.

"So let the most just ruler pass," said King Mallika's driver. "My master conquers the fierce with his mighty sword and the wicked with greater wickedness."

King Brahmadatta's driver smiled. "Then I see it is settled," he said. "For my master conquers the fierce with calmness and the wicked with goodness."

At these words, King Mallika's chariot driver recognised true justice and made way for the wise, peaceful King Brahmadatta.

SEPTEMBER

SEPTEMBER
AUTUMN-TIME

WHY THE EVERGREENS KEEP THEIR LEAVES
AN AMERICAN STORY

The autumn days were cold, winter was coming. All the birds flew away to a warmer place, but one little bird had a broken wing and couldn't fly. The little bird shivered. "Maybe the trees will keep me warm through the winter," he thought and so he hopped to the edge of the wood.

He came to a silver birch. "Beautiful birch tree," said the little bird, "will you keep me warm in your branches?"

The silver birch rustled. "I have my leaves to look after," she said. "I can't look after you too!"

The little bird hopped on to the great oak tree. "Mighty oak," he said, "will you keep me warm in your branches?"

The oak tree groaned. "I don't want any-one eating my acorns," he said.

So the little bird hopped on, to where the willow tree grew.

"Gentle willow," he said, "will you keep me warm in your branches?"

The willow shuddered. "I never welcome strangers," she said.

The little bird shook his cold feathers and sighed. "Who will help me?" he murmured.

"You can live on my branches," said the spruce. "I'll keep you warm all winter."

"I'll shelter you from the wind," said the pine tree.

"And you may eat my berries," said the juniper.

So, the grateful bird hopped onto the branches of the spruce and found himself a warm place.

That night, the North Wind blustered through the wood and blew the leaves from the trees. But he left the trees that were taking care of the little bird.

And the kindness of the spruce, the pine and the juniper is never forgotten; for while the other trees lose their leaves each autumn, those three always remain green.

SEPTEMBER
AUTUMN-TIME

THE GIFTS OF
THE NORTH WIND

A NORWEGIAN STORY

Greta and her mother were poor, with only an old hen to lay eggs and a stony garden to grow vegetables.

One winter's day, the North Wind gusted around their house, rattling the shutters. "What will become of us," sighed Greta's mother, "without money to buy food or firewood?"

"Don't worry, mother," said Greta, "I'll make some hot soup." But when she went to the cupboard there wasn't even a carrot to cook. Determined not to be defeated, Greta took a dish and went out to the storehouse, where she found a few handfuls of flour at the bottom of the flour jar. "At least this will make a warm little cake for mother," she thought.

Greta was carrying the dish down the steps of the storehouse when the North Wind whooshed past, blowing the flour right out of the dish and away.

"Hey," cried Greta, "bring back that flour!" She was so angry that she grabbed her coat from the house and set off after the wind.

Greta followed a trail of scattered leaves and broken branches until, at last, she came to a cave at the foot of a mountain – the home of the North Wind.

"Good day," said the North Wind. "What can I do for you?"

"Good day," said Greta. "Can you kindly return the flour you took from us, or my poor mother and I shall have nothing to eat?"

"I'm sorry," said the North Wind, "I don't have your flour. Take this cloth instead. It will give you all the food you want. Just spread it on the table and say 'Feed me!'."

"That's a good exchange," thought Greta, so she took the cloth, thanked the North Wind and started for home.

But Greta had travelled too far to get back in a day, so she stopped for the night at an inn.

Sitting down at a table, she spread the cloth and said "Feed me!" At once, the cloth was covered with dishes of delicious food.

When the innkeeper saw this, he winked to his wife. That night, while Greta was asleep, the innkeeper's wife swapped the cloth for an old pillowcase.

The next morning Greta hurried home. "Now you shall have the best meal of your life, Mother," she promised. But when she spread the pillowcase on the table and said the words, nothing appeared.

"That's not right!" said Greta crossly and she took it straight back to the North Wind.

"Good day," said the North Wind. "Are you still hungry?"

"This cloth has shrunk to the size of a pillowcase and won't give any food at all," said Greta.

"Then take this goat," said the North Wind. "When you say 'Make gold!' it will give you as much gold as you need."

"That's a fine exchange," thought Greta, so she took the goat, thanked the North Wind and set off for home.

On the way, Greta stopped at the inn as before. That night, she ordered the best meal. When it was time to pay, Greta said to the goat "Make gold!" and a dozen gold coins fell from its mouth.

SEPTEMBER

The innkeeper saw this and smiled at his wife.

That night, while Greta was asleep, the innkeeper swapped her goat for a scrawny old goat of his own.

When Greta returned home the next day she brought her mother out to see the goat. "Now we shall be able to buy as much food and firewood as we need," she promised. But when Greta told the goat to make gold, it just bleated at them crossly.

"That's not right!" said Greta and she took it straight back to the North Wind.

"Good day," said the North Wind as Greta tugged the reluctant goat into the cave. "That's not the goat I gave you!"

"No," said Greta. "There's not a gold coin in it."

"Then take this broom," said the North Wind. "If you say 'Sweep, broom!' it will sweep your troubles away."

"That's a fair exchange," thought Greta, "and I think I know where to find the cause of my troubles." So she took the broom, thanked the North Wind and went back to the inn.

That night, the innkeeper gave Greta a fine supper and the softest bed.

"That broom must be worth having," he whispered to his wife. When he thought Greta was asleep he crept into her room to swap it for his own.

But Greta was waiting. "Sweep broom!" she said. At once, the broom leapt to life and beat the innkeeper till he ran wailing down the stairs. Out rushed his wife and the broom beat her too.

"Help! Help!" they cried. "Take your cloth! Take your goat!"

"Well, that's an excellent exchange," laughed Greta and she left them the broom and went home to her mother.

OCTOBER

OCTOBER 16TH
WORLD FOOD DAY

THE RAJA
AND THE RICE
AN INDIAN STORY

Once, there was a Raja, who was content with the pleasures of his palace and never travelled around the country to see how his people lived.

There came a year when the rice harvest was bad. As usual, the farmers brought rice to fill the palace storehouse, so the Raja could enjoy his fine banquets, but there wasn't enough left to feed the people, who had no choice but to beg for food in the streets.

One morning, an old man came to the palace with a present for the Raja.

"I've invented a new board game, your highness," he said. "It's a battle game of great skill. I call it 'chess'." The Raja loved games, at once he was intrigued. The old man showed him the carved chess pieces. "The finest piece is Your Highness himself," he explained, "riding on your favourite elephant!"

The Raja was delighted. "You must teach me how to play this marvellous new game," he said and the old man agreed.

Day after day, the old man made his way to the palace, through streets crowded with starving beggars and hungry children, to teach the Raja how to play chess. Before long, the Raja learnt the rules and became skilled at the game.

"I am very pleased with this present," he said to the old man. "I have taught my wife and all my family to play. What can I give you as a gift of thanks?"

The old man scratched his beard and gazed out of the palace window thoughtfully.

"I would like some rice, Your Highness," he said.

"Rice!" the Raja laughed. "Look around you, my friend," he said. "I have fine paintings and jewels and fabulous singing birds. Choose yourself a treasure. I promise you may have whatever you wish."

The old man bowed humbly. "Rice will be thanks enough for the chess game," he said. "If you please, one grain on the first square of the board, two on the second square, four on the next and so on, doubling up each time across the board."

The Raja thought this was an odd request, but he called for a bowl of rice and began putting the grains on the board himself. To his surprise, as he began doubling up, he soon needed so many grains of rice that they wouldn't fit on the squares. "Bring a casket to put it in," he asked the servants. "And more rice!"

The rice filled the casket and then a sack, then another. By the end of the second row of squares, the Raja had to count thirty-two thousand, seven hundred and sixty-eight grains and, for the next square, twice as much.

All that day and the next, the servants brought rice and the Raja counted. The corridors of the palace were filled with sacks piled high, until there was not one single grain left in the storehouse.

"Fetch more rice from the farmers," said the Raja wearily. "I must keep my promise." But the old man shook his head.

"Didn't you know there's a famine in the land, Your Highness?" he said. "There is no rice to feed even the hungriest child."

At these words the Raja was troubled. "No child should go hungry," he said, sorrowfully. "I see I have neglected my people. But now I have given all my rice to you."

The old man smiled. "I never wanted it for myself, Your Highness," he said. "I only ask you to give a bowl of rice to every hungry person outside your palace door and then we will all be rewarded."

OCTOBER

OCTOBER 16TH
WORLD FOOD DAY

WHY THE BANANAS BELONG TO THE MONKEY
A BRAZILIAN STORY

Long ago, when the world had just been made, there was an old woman who had a big garden full of banana trees. As it was difficult for her to pick the bananas, she asked the biggest monkey in the forest to help, knowing how much he liked to eat them.

"If you pick all my bananas, I'll let you keep half of them," she said.

The biggest monkey agreed. As soon as the bananas were ready, he picked every one. Then he divided them into two piles – the long, fat bananas for himself and the small, wrinkled ones for the old woman.

When the old woman realised she'd been made a fool of, she was very angry. "I'll show that greedy monkey a good trick," she muttered and she lay awake all night thinking of what to do.

Next morning, she took some wax and made the figure of a boy. Then she dressed him up, put a basket of bananas on his head and stood him by the side of the road.

Before long, the biggest monkey swung by. Although he now had plenty of bananas, he was so greedy that he wanted more.

"Give me a banana, fruit seller," he said. But the boy didn't answer.

The biggest monkey asked again, in a louder voice. "Give me a banana, fruit seller. You've got plenty."

Still the boy said nothing. The biggest monkey began to get cross.

"If you don't give me a banana, I'll knock that basket off your head and help myself!" he said.

As before, the boy just stared at him. So, the biggest monkey reached out to knock the basket off the boy's head, but, to his surprise, his hand stuck fast in the wax.

OCTOBER

94

"Let me go and give me a banana!" cried the biggest monkey. He reached out with his other hand and that stuck too.

The biggest monkey pulled and pulled but couldn't free himself. Now he was so cross with the boy that he gave him a sharp kick. But his foot stuck to the wax and he sat down with a bump.

"Let me go or I'll knock you over and have all the bananas for myself!" shouted the biggest monkey and he kicked hard with his other foot, which stuck in the wax too.

Now the biggest monkey tugged and pulled so much that all the bananas toppled out of the basket onto the path, but he couldn't reach a single one. Then he howled and yelled and made such a noise that all the other monkeys in the forest came running.

"Unstick me!" cried the biggest monkey. "I've been tricked!" All the monkeys of the forest tugged and pulled, but they couldn't free him from the little wax boy. Then the very smallest monkey had an idea.

"If we climb to the top of a tree and stand on each other's shoulders, with the loudest monkey on top," he said, "then he could shout up to the sun and ask him to melt the little wax boy."

So that is what they did, and the sun shone his hottest rays down on the little boy and melted his wax body, so that the biggest monkey could pull his hands and feet free.

When the old woman saw how clever the monkeys had been, she decided to give up growing bananas. "I'm going to move to a place where I can grow beans that I can pick myself," she said.

Ever since that day, the monkeys have thought that all the bananas belong to them.

OCTOBER

OCTOBER
DIWALI

RAMA AND SITA
AN INDIAN STORY

Prince Rama was the eldest son of King Dashratha and much loved by his father. When Rama married a beautiful princess called Sita, the whole kingdom celebrated with joy.

"Now you have a wife, I shall give you my crown," said the king. "I see you will be a fair and wise ruler."

But Rama's stepmother wanted her own son to sit on the throne. She tricked the king into agreeing to this and made him banish Rama from the kingdom for fourteen years.

Rama and Sita left the palace to find a new home and Rama's young brother, Lakshmana, went with them. They built a house in the forest and there they lived a simple, happy life together.

One day, Sita spotted a golden deer in the forest. She asked Rama to catch it for her as a companion. Rama left Lakshmana to look after Sita and went to hunt for the deer. Shortly afterwards, Sita heard Rama cry out in alarm.

"Go to your brother," she told Lakshmana. "He is in trouble!"

Lakshmana was reluctant to leave Sita alone, but she insisted. First, he drew a circle around the house with his arrow. "Stay inside this circle and you'll be safe," he promised her.

While he was gone, a bent old man staggered up to the house. With a piteous cry, he stumbled and fell. Without thinking, Sita rushed to help him. But as soon as she stepped out of the circle, the old man disappeared. In his place rose the great demon king, Ravana!

"Now, I shall have you for my wife!" cried Ravana and he swept her up into his chariot.

As Ravana's winged chariot lurched into the sky, Sita thought quickly. She dropped a trail of jewellery for Rama to follow.

When Rama returned and found Sita gone, he realised that he and his brother had been lured away with a trick. Rama

searched desperately for his wife and found the glittering trail, but the jewels soon ran out. Hurrying on through the forest, he met Hanuman, the monkey king.

Rama had once helped Hanuman, so when the monkey king heard that the princess was missing, he offered to help in return. "My monkeys will find Sita," he promised.

Hanuman called all the monkeys of the world and they came, with their friends, the bears, to search for the princess. But it was Hanuman himself who discovered that she was held prisoner by Ravana, on an island far from the shore.

"How can we rescue her?" said Rama, gazing across the water.

The monkeys and bears talked together awhile, then they picked up rocks and began to build a bridge to the island. Rama and Lakshmana joined in and all the animals came out of the forest to help. The bridge grew, rock by rock, until Rama could lead his animal army across to the island.

When they reached Ravana's island there was a fierce battle. The animals fought the demons bravely. Rama faced Ravana and shot an arrow that sliced off his head. But when the head fell, another grew in its place. Nine times Rama shot an arrow and nine times Ravana's head grew back, until Hanuman shouted "Aim lower, friend!"

Rama lowered his aim and hit Ravana's chest. At last, the demon king fell dead to the ground.

Rama and Sita were happily reunited.

"I shall never send you into the forest again, my love," said Sita.

"We don't need to return to the forest," said Rama. "Fourteen years have passed now. We can go home, at last, to our own kingdom."

And so, Rama, Sita and Lakshmana left the demon's island, and as they walked together they saw a thousand sparkling lights; for everyone had been awaiting their return and had lit lamps along the way, to guide their beloved prince and princess home.

OCTOBER

OCTOBER 31ST
HALLOWEEN

THE BURIED MOON
AN ENGLISH STORY

Long ago, wicked things haunted the watery marshlands. On dark nights, eerie lanterns would lure travellers away from the paths, where slithering creatures in dangerous bogs and murky pools waited to drag them to a gruesome fate.

The Moon heard tales of these terrors and wished to know if they were true. So, she wrapped herself in a black cloak, pulled the hood over her head, and stepped down to the marshland.

Cautiously, the Moon crept through the marsh. At the edge of a slimy pool her foot slipped. She reached out for a branch to save herself from falling, but, to her horror, woody fingers twined around her wrists and gripped her tight. She was trapped!

The Moon tugged and twisted, but couldn't free herself. Then a frightened voice whimpered in the darkness; a man had strayed from the path and was squelching through the bog, heading for a lantern light he hoped was a sign of safety. Only the Moon heard the slobbering creatures waiting to grab him.

At once, she shook the hood from her shining hair, casting bright moonbeams across the marsh and the crawling terrors shrieked and squirmed back into the bog.

The man cried with joy at seeing the path once more. He hurried back to safety with little more than a glance over his shoulder at the light that had saved him.

Now the Moon was alone without any hope of help. She sank to her knees and the hood fell over her head once more.

But she had given herself away. As soon as it was dark again, the wicked creatures emerged from the bog and clamoured around her, screeching and plucking at her with bony fingers. They

hated the Moon's light. After a squabble, they decided to bury her deep in the pool at the foot of the tree and roll a huge stone on top of her. Intending to return to gloat, they left a ghostly lantern to mark the place.

Days passed and the Moon didn't appear in the sky. The people who lived by the marsh grew fearful and the creatures of the bog became bold, creeping up to their houses at night to claw at the windows.

Nobody could guess what had happened to the Moon, until, one evening, a traveller at an inn told his story.

"I believe I saw her!" he said. "I was lost in the marsh on a dark night when a light, soft as a moonbeam, showed me the path and saved me from certain death."

When the men of the marshland heard this, they hurried to the wise woman of the village to ask her advice.

The wise woman consulted her brew-pot. "Tonight, you must go to the marsh," she said. "Look for a coffin, a cross and a candle. There you may find the Moon. But first, put stones in your mouths – for you mustn't speak a word until you are safe home again."

The men waited for dusk and then did as she said. They picked their way nervously around the bogs until they found the huge stone, rising from the water like a coffin. Looking up, they saw two crossed branches and the ghostly lantern, flickering like a candle.

Without a word, they lifted the stone and, to their relief, the marsh was flooded with light. The grateful Moon leapt out of the water, back into the sky.

Ever since that night, the Moon has shone more brightly for the people of the marshland than anyone else.

OCTOBER

OCTOBER 31ST
HALLOWEEN

THE SHORTEST GHOST STORY IN THE WORLD

AN ENGLISH STORY

One night, a man woke up in a fright. He reached for the matches, to light a candle... and the matches were put into his hand.

NOVEMBER

NOVEMBER
THANKSGIVING

HOW THE PINE-TREE CHIEF GOT HIS NAME
AN IROQUOIS STORY

It was a bright day in autumn-time and the forest was busy with birds. A boy was running along the woodland trail in his new moccasins, happy to feel the warm sun on his face, when he noticed something hanging on the branch of a bush. He stopped and gazed in wonder – for it was a little cradle board, no bigger than his thumb.

The boy had never seen such a small cradle board. He gently lifted it down and held it in his hands. To his surprise, a tiny baby peeped out. The baby stared up at him and laughed.

The boy smiled. "You need someone to take care of you, little one," he said. "I'll take you home to mother. She has nine children already but there will be room for you."

The boy tucked the little cradle board carefully inside his tunic and turned back towards the trail. But no matter how hard he tried to walk ahead, his feet would not do as he wished and he found he could only walk around the bush.

Three times round the bush he walked, until he heard a sharp, fearful cry. A little woman, no taller than a rabbit, came running down the trail, with tears in her eyes.

She held her arms out to the boy. "Give me back my baby," she pleaded.

The boy realised at once that it was the power of the mother's love for her baby that had kept him from walking away. He lifted the cradle board out of his tunic and carefully put it on the mother's back. "Now your baby is safe, where she belongs," he said.

The little woman was very grateful. She beckoned to the boy to take off his necklace of beads, then she took a bright stone from her bag and threaded it onto the necklace.

"We little people give this stone to one who protects the weak," she said. "It will bring you

whatever you want. You are kind and good — always wear this stone and one day you will become a mighty chief."

Then the nimble little woman jumped into the branches of an oak tree, with her baby on her back, and disappeared.

The boy ran on down the trail, proudly wearing the bright stone, and by the time he reached home, he'd caught plenty of food for supper.

From that day, just as the little woman had promised, he had good luck in everything; if he went fishing, he caught plenty of fat fish, if he planted corn, it grew tall and fine. He could run faster than all the other boys, shoot an arrow higher and skim a snake-stick further across the snow.

"This boy wears the good-luck stone," said the old people of his tribe, and they decided to call him Luck-in-all-moons.

As time passed, Luck-in-all-moons grew tall and strong. He looked after his mother and his eight brothers and sisters and always protected the weak. Many people saw his good deeds and his kind heart.

One day, just as the little woman had promised, the elders of his tribe decided to make him a chief.

"Luck-in-all-moons, you serve our people well," they said. "You stand strong and straight, like the pine tree, and your feet are planted deep in wisdom. You shall be called the Pine-tree Chief."

Then the Pine-tree Chief felt the stone shine brightly at his neck. He remembered the tiny baby, no bigger than his thumb, and he smiled, gratefully.

NOVEMBER

NOVEMBER
THANKSGIVING

THE GIFT OF A COW-TAIL SWITCH

A WEST AFRICAN STORY

In a village in West Africa, there lived a great hunter who had three sons. Early one morning, he took up his spear, hung a bow and quiver of arrows across his back, and set off to go hunting. As his wife watched him walk away out of the village, she smiled and rubbed her belly, for she was soon to have another child.

However, by sunset, the hunter hadn't returned. His wife and sons waited for him all night and the following day. They waited the next night and the day after that, but still he didn't appear.

Then the wife said to her sons, "Go after your father and find him."

So the three sons went to look for their father, but although they searched far and wide, they found no sign of him and returned with no news.

As weeks passed, the woman and her sons thought about the hunter, but they stopped speaking of him.

As months passed, they stopped thinking about the hunter, and so his memory faded from their minds.

Then the baby was born and it was a girl. She soon grew from a baby into a child. She learnt to walk and then to speak. To everyone's surprise, the first words she said were: "Where is my father?"

Her mother gasped. "How could we have forgotten him?" she cried and she sent her three sons to search for him again.

The three sons searched far and wide and farther still. At last, they found a scatter of bones, with their father's spear, his bow and quiver of arrows lying beside them.

NOVEMBER

The first son knelt down and breathed on his father's bones. The bones began to twitch. Slowly, they rolled towards each other and joined themselves into a skeleton.

The second son knelt down and breathed on the skeleton. His father's muscles and flesh grew back again and covered the bones.

The third son knelt down and breathed on the body. The hunter inhaled deeply, then he sat up and opened his eyes.

"What happened?" he asked, as if he'd woken from a long sleep.

"You were dead," said his three sons. "Now you can come home."

The hunter and his sons returned home and there was great celebration and a fine feast that night.

When the meal was over, the hunter sat by the fire. He took out his knife and began to carve a piece of wood. The three sons watched silently as he carved animals and birds and trees and flowers in the firelight. None of them had ever seen such a wonder.

When the carving was finished, the hunter braided a fine black cow's tail and fixed it onto the wooden handle.

"What is it?" asked his daughter.

"It is a cow-tail switch," said the hunter, "to keep the flies away. I have made it as a gift for the one who brought me back to life."

Then the three sons spoke up.

"It was me who brought you to life, father," said the first son. "I gathered your scattered bones."

"No, I brought you to life," said the second son. "I put flesh on your body."

"I gave you breath," said the third son. "There is no life without breath."

But the hunter beckoned his daughter close. "This is the one who brought me back to life," he said, "for she remembered me, and as long as a man is remembered, he is never truly dead." And he gave his daughter the precious gift of the beautiful cow-tail switch.

NOVEMBER

NOVEMBER 5TH
BONFIRE NIGHT

HOW GRANDMOTHER SPIDER BROUGHT FIRE
A CHOCTAW STORY

When the Earth was first made there was no sun or moon in the sky, not even a star. The world was cold and dark. Life was hard for the birds and animals and people.

One day, Raven called everyone to a great gathering.

"I have heard there is something called 'fire' on the other side of the world," he said. "It makes light and heat."

"What is light and heat?" asked Fox.

"I don't know," said Raven, "but if they have it on the other side of the world then we should have it too."

"Perhaps we can share some of this fire," Fox suggested and the others agreed. But who would fetch it?

"I'm a great hunter," said Possum, "I'll find the fire and bring some back in my thick, bushy tail." So the gathering agreed that Possum should go.

Possum journeyed to the other side of the world and found the bright fire. He put a tiny piece under his tail, and set off for home. But the little flame grew. It quickly burnt all the hair on his tail and then it went out.

Possum returned to the gathering without any fire and, to this day, all possums have bare tails.

"Let me try," said Buzzard. "I will be swift on my great wings."

Buzzard flew to the other side of the world and found the bright fire. He put a small piece

among his head feathers to carry it home. But he soon smelt smoke. Flames burnt off his head feathers and then they went out.

Buzzard returned to the gathering without any fire and, to this day, all buzzards have bald, red heads.

Then a tiny voice spoke from the back of the gathering. "Let me fetch the fire." It was Grandmother Spider.

"Do you think you can succeed when Possum and Buzzard have failed?" asked Raven.

"Yes," said Grandmother Spider. "I may be small but I have many skills."

So the gathering agreed that she should try.

First, Grandmother Spider went down to the river and found some clay, which she shaped into a pot with a well-fitting lid. Next, she took a thorn and made a small hole in the lid. Then she put the pot on her back and fixed it with a thread. When everything was ready, she spun a web all the way to the other side of the world.

The bright fire was easy to find. Grand-mother Spider put a tiny piece inside the pot and closed the lid tight. Then she followed her way back along the web to the gathering.

Nobody noticed that Grandmother Spider had returned, for the light of the fire was hidden in the pot. But when she took off the lid, the fire blazed.

Everyone at the gathering was amazed. For the first time they saw each other and felt warmth on their fur and feathers and skin.

"Who shall look after this precious fire?" asked Raven. The animals shook their heads, for they had seen Possum's burnt tail. The birds shook their heads, for they had seen Buzzard's burnt head. But the people stepped forward.

"We'll take care of it," they said.

So Grandmother Spider taught the people how to feed the fire to keep it alive, and how to circle it with stones, to keep it safe.

Then she spun a web high up into the sky, and threw sparks from her pot to make the sun and the moon and the stars, so there was light and warmth for all the world.

NOVEMBER

NOVEMBER 26TH
NATIONAL TREE WEEK

THE WOODCUTTER AND THE WOLF
A FRENCH STORY

One day, the woodcutter's wife sent him to the market, to buy two loaves of black bread. He was walking home through the forest with the rings of bread over his arms, when a huge grey wolf stepped out onto the path.

The wolf stared at the woodcutter and growled.

"What shall I do?" thought the woodcutter. "This wolf looks thin and hungry. He'll surely eat me!" Then he had an idea.

"Here, wolf," he said, "try this good bread." He broke off a piece and threw it to the wolf. As soon as the wolf began to eat, the woodcutter hurried past.

But moments later he heard the wolf tramping after him. The woodcutter broke off another piece of bread, threw it behind him and ran on. Again and again he threw bread to the wolf, delaying him just enough to keep ahead, until, at last, he reached the edge of the forest and saw his wife waiting for him at their cottage door.

He stumbled up to the door, gasping for breath.

"What's the matter?" asked his wife. "And where are the loaves I asked you to buy?" The woodcutter pointed to the wolf tramping out of the forest.

"A wolf stole our bread!" cried his wife.

"No, I gave it to him," explained the woodcutter.

"Why should we waste good bread on a wicked wolf," said his wife crossly. "Now we'll have nothing to eat with our soup!" And she stamped inside.

The woodcutter looked at the hungry wolf, standing at the cottage gate.

"At least we have soup," he said. "You might as well have this bread," and he threw the last piece of crust to the wolf. Then he followed his wife inside.

NOVEMBER

As they ate their soup, the woodcutter's wife moaned and moaned about the wolf, wishing that he would suffer a terrible fate. She didn't notice the grey shadow outside the window, listening in.

A few months later, having worked hard and saved his money, the woodcutter returned to the market, hoping to buy a cow. However, to his dismay, the cows were too expensive.

He was about to return home empty-handed, when a tall stranger dressed in grey appeared before him.

"I have many cows," said the stranger. "I'll gladly give you one as a gift."

The woodcutter was amazed and grateful. He chose himself a fine cow. "But why are you doing me such a kindness?" he asked.

The stranger smiled. "Once, you showed kindness to a hungry wolf," he said. "I always repay what I am given in equal measure. And here, too, is a gift for your wife." Then he gave the woodcutter a little box and went on his way.

The woodcutter set off home. As he led the cow through the forest he began to grow curious to know what was inside the box. "There can be no harm in having a peep," he thought, "my wife will surely show me." So he tied up the cow and sat down beneath a larch tree.

As soon as he opened the box a tall flame leapt out and set fire to the tree. The woodcutter jumped up and dropped the box. "Thank goodness my wife didn't open it, or she'd have been burnt to a cinder!" he said and he hurried home with the cow.

Behind him, the blazing larch soon set the whole forest alight and it was burnt to ashes.

But the woodcutter now had a fine milk cow, and so he became a cheesemaker, and he and his wife lived happily ever after.

NOVEMBER

NOVEMBER 26TH
NATIONAL TREE WEEK

THE TREE OF MAGICAL LEAVES
A CHINESE STORY

Many years ago, all the people in China had to pay money to the emperor. Every village had a tax collector, who went from house to house collecting the money and sent it to the palace. But in one village, the tax collector was a wicked, dishonest man.

This greedy tax collector would often keep half the money for himself. Worse still, if people didn't have enough to pay him, he would demand something else instead — their animals, their furniture, sometimes even their house, and he'd threaten to lock them up if they refused. Everyone was afraid of the tax collector and kept out of his way.

One day, a young man in the next village heard how the people were afraid and he had an idea. He dug up a little pear tree in his garden and planted it in a pot, then he carried the tree to the tax collector's village.

The tax collector was always watching out for strangers so that he could trick them into giving him money. He soon spotted the young man with the tree and stopped him in the road.

"No one can walk through this village without paying tax to the emperor," he said to the young man. "You must give me some money!"

"But I don't have any money," said the young man. "I only have this magical tree."

"Magical tree?" muttered the tax collector. "Hmm. What does it do?"

"The leaves can make you invisible," explained the young man. "You just have to pick one and put it on your forehead."

The tax collector's eyes lit up. "Well," he said, "if you have no money, the emperor will accept your tree instead," and he took the magic tree for himself.

NOVEMBER

112

When he got home, the tax collector immediately picked a leaf from the pear tree and put it on his forehead, then he went out to the village square to test whether he was invisible or not.

There were plenty of people in the village square, but not one of them looked at the tax collector; they didn't want to attract his attention in case he asked them for money.

"I think it works!" he thought excitedly. He tried helping himself to some bread from a market stall. The baker pretended not to notice. The tax collector pinched an apple, then a hat, then he stole a rug, right in front of the carpet seller. Everyone looked away and pretended he wasn't there.

The tax collector laughed. "It does work!" he thought happily. "Now I'm invisible I can take anything I like!"

At that moment, the emperor himself came riding through the village. On the back of his carriage hung a beautiful bird in a golden cage that had been given to him as a present.

The greedy tax collector rubbed his hands with delight. "That golden bird cage would make me a wealthy man!" Without a care, he walked right up to the carriage and took it.

The emperor's guard spotted him at once. "Thief!" he cried. "How dare you steal from the emperor?"

The tax collector realised he'd been tricked! "Somebody gave me a tree of magical leaves," he blubbered. "I thought I was invisible."

The emperor stepped down from his carriage. "You are not fit to be my tax collector," he said. "A thief belongs in the palace dungeon."

Then everyone in the village came to watch the wicked tax collector being taken away.

The young man sitting outside the inn smiled to himself.

"Now the tax collector really is going to disappear!" he said.

NOVEMBER

NOVEMBER 30TH

ST ANDREW'S DAY

CONALL AND THE THUNDER HAG

A SCOTTISH STORY

One winter's day, the Thunder Hag came riding across the sea to Scotland, in her black chariot, drawn by four fierce red hounds.

Suddenly, the sky grew dark as night. The hounds howled as the Thunder Hag raced over hills and moors, hurling fireballs that set the forests ablaze. Everyone ran from the smoke and flames in terror!

The next day, the hag returned, burning trees and setting the dry heather alight. The king sent his warriors to slay her, but when they saw the teeth of her fierce hounds they fled.

On the third day, the Thunder Hag returned again, causing destruction across the land. The king sent for the fearless hero, Conall Curlew.

"I need your help, noble Conall," said the King.

Conall agreed to rid the kingdom of the Thunder Hag. "If I don't defeat her today," he said, "I may defeat her tomorrow."

Conall climbed a mountain and waited for the Thunder Hag. But when she came, she was hidden by the black clouds around her chariot and he could do nothing.

The next day, he went into the fields and separated all the lambs and calves and foals from their mothers. Then he returned to the mountain top.

Before long, the Thunder Hag arrived. She heard the terrible noise of the sheep and cattle and mares, crying desperately for their young ones, and was so curious to see what could be making such a woeful sound that she peered out of her cloud.

At once, brave Conall threw his spear. The Thunder Hag screamed and fell back in her chariot.

"Fly west!" she cried to her hounds, and she was never seen again.

DECEMBER

DECEMBER 10TH
HUMAN RIGHTS DAY

THE BELL OF ATRI
AN ITALIAN STORY

A long time ago, in Italy, there was a good king, who wanted all the people in his kingdom to be treated fairly.

He asked for a tower to be built in the town of Atri and a fine bell to be hung in it.

When the bell-tower was finished, the King came to see it. All the people of Atri gathered in the market-square.

"This bell is for everyone in the town," the King explained. "The bell rope is long enough for any man, woman or child to reach. If someone treats you badly, you only have to ring the bell and one of my judges will come straightaway to set things right and see that justice is done."

The people of Atri were very grateful to the King.

Sure enough, as the King promised, a judge came whenever the bell was rung. Every injustice was put right at once, even the troubles of the smallest child.

As years went by, people learnt that it was best to be kind and fair towards each other, and the bell of Atri was hardly rung at all.

One morning, the Mayor of the town was walking past the tower and noticed that the bell rope had frayed away at the end. "We must replace this rope," the Mayor told his secretary. "The King insisted it should be long enough for every man, woman and child to reach."

"But there isn't a rope-maker in Atri," said the secretary. "I shall have to send for a new one to be made elsewhere."

"Then that's what we'll do," agreed the Mayor. "In the meantime, I have a long grapevine growing in my garden. It's very strong. You can cut a piece and repair the bell rope with that, and make sure it hangs low enough for the smallest child to reach."

So, the secretary cut a length of the grapevine in the Mayor's garden and attached it firmly to the bell rope.

The very next morning, everyone in the town was woken by the bell ringing loudly.

DECEMBER

They dressed themselves and came rushing into the square. To their surprise, they saw a lame old horse, trying to eat the leaves of the grapevine. Each time he tugged at the vine, he pulled on the bell.

The Judge arrived, still buttoning up his coat. "Who rang the bell so urgently?" he asked.

"It's a bony old horse looking for a bite to eat," said a woman in the crowd. "Look at his dirty coat and skinny ribs. I've never seen such a starved, neglected animal."

"Who does he belong to?" asked the Judge.

The town postman stepped forward. "I know this horse," he said. "He used to belong to the old soldier who lives on the hill. He carried the soldier into battle many years ago and even saved his master's life. When they came home from the war, he worked on the soldier's farm, until he was too old and weak to pull the plough. But instead of giving him a stable and a well-earned rest, his master turned him away and left him wandering without a home, living on whatever he could find to eat at the roadside."

The Judge listened with a frown. "Bring the old soldier here," he demanded.

The old soldier was brought to the market-square. He was very puzzled to see the whole town gathered around a half-starved, miserable looking horse, munching on a grape-vine.

"Is it true that you unfairly abandoned this horse, who served you well for many years?" asked the Judge. Then the old soldier looked again and recognised the poor creature. He nodded and hung his head in shame.

"I order that you take him home, give him a comfortable stable and feed him well," said the Judge. "He has a right to be cared for kindly until the end of his days."

The old soldier agreed. "I see that I have treated you most unfairly, my friend," he said to the horse. "I promise you'll be well looked after from now on."

The Judge smiled with satisfaction. "The King will be pleased to hear that even a horse may pull the bell of Atri, to see that justice is done!" he said.

Then the old horse nuzzled his master happily and the good people of Atri cheered.

DECEMBER

DECEMBER
MIDWINTER

EAST OF THE SUN, WEST OF THE MOON
A SCANDINAVIAN STORY

Once upon a time, there lived a man and his wife, who were so poor that their children had no shoes and often went to bed hungry.

One winter's evening, the man heard three taps on the window. He went outside, and there was a white bear.

"Good evening," said the bear.

"Good evening, Bear," said the man. "Can I help you?"

"I can help you," said the bear. "If you give me one of your daughters, I will make you rich."

The man thought about his hungry children, but he loved them all and couldn't send one away. "Thank you, Bear," he said. "But I cannot give you one of my daughters."

"So be it," said the bear sadly and he padded away through the snow. Suddenly he heard a voice.

"Wait, Bear!" It was the youngest daughter, Eva, who had been listening to his words.

"I'll come with you," she said, "if you will make my father rich."

"Then climb onto my back," said the bear. "My thick fur will keep you warm."

The bear carried Eva through the forest, to a cave. Inside, there was a warm fire and a delicious dinner waiting. When she'd eaten, the bear showed Eva to a beautiful room with a four-poster bed and feather pillows.

After she'd climbed into bed and snuffed out the candle, Eva heard somebody come into the room and lie down on the rug beside her.

"Is that you, Bear?" she whispered, but all she heard was a gentle snore. In the morning, she was alone.

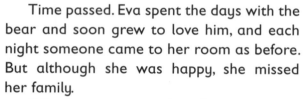

Time passed. Eva spent the days with the bear and soon grew to love him, and each night someone came to her room as before. But although she was happy, she missed her family.

"I'll take you to visit them," said the bear, "but don't listen to any of your mother's advice – it will bring us bad luck."

The bear took Eva to a grand house, where her family now had everything they wished for and there was a joyful reunion. Eva told them about the bear and the visitor who came to her room at night.

"Your visitor might be a troll!" said her mother. "My advice is to light a candle while he sleeps and have a look at him."

That night, back in the bear's cave, Eva remembered her mother's advice, but she forgot the bear's warning. When her visitor was asleep on the rug, she lit a candle.

Beside her bed lay a handsome prince, with hair as white as the bear. As she leant over him, three drops of candlewax fell onto his shirt.

The prince woke up. "Oh Eva, what have you done?" he cried. "My stepmother has bewitched me. I had to live with you for a year without being seen to break the spell. Now I must marry her daughter, the troll princess!"

Eva begged him not to go, but it was no use.

"Where will I find you?" she cried.

"In a castle, east of the sun and west of the moon," said the prince. "That is all I know."

Then the prince and the cave were gone.

Eva set off to find the castle. She walked for many days, until she met an old woman, holding a golden apple.

"Do you know the way to a castle, east of the sun, west of the moon?" asked Eva.

"No," said the old woman. "But have this golden apple."

Eva walked on and met another old woman, holding a golden carding comb. She asked the same question.

"I don't know the castle," said the old woman. "But have this golden carding comb."

A little further, Eva met a third old

woman, sitting at a golden spinning wheel. Once more, she asked how to find the castle.

"Only the North Wind knows," said the old woman and she gave Eva the golden spinning wheel.

Eva searched until she found the North Wind.

"I can take you there," boomed the North Wind. "Hold on tight!" Then he blew Eva high into the air, east of the sun, west of the moon, and tumbled her onto the grass beneath the castle window.

The troll princess looked out of the window.

"What do you want for that golden ball?" she said.

"Let me stay the night with the prince," said Eva.

The troll princess agreed. But first, she gave the prince a sleeping potion, so that Eva couldn't wake him.

The next day, the troll princess asked for the golden carding comb. Once again, Eva asked to stay with the prince. As before, she couldn't wake him.

The third day, the troll princess asked for the golden spinning wheel. This time, the prince, who'd grown suspicious of the potion, only pretended to take it. Eva was filled with joy to find him awake and told him all that had happened.

"Now you can save me!" said the prince.

Next morning, he told his stepmother that he would marry the girl who could wash the candlewax off his shirt.

The troll princess grabbed his shirt, but she only made it filthy. So he called for Eva. As soon as she touched the shirt it became clean again.

"This is the girl I shall marry!" said the prince. Then his stepmother and the troll princess flew into such a rage that they exploded on the spot.

DECEMBER

DECEMBER 25TH
CHRISTMAS

UNCLE MARTIN
A FRENCH STORY

It was Christmas Eve. Old Uncle Martin, the shoemaker, stepped outside to gaze at the falling snow. He remembered how he'd loved Christmas when his wife was alive and his own children were young.

"Those were happy times," he sighed. "But though I'm alone now, it is still a special day."

He went inside, lit his lamp and made himself a pot of coffee. Then he took his Bible from the shelf and found the Christmas story.

He read how Jesus was born in a stable, because there was nowhere else for Mary and Joseph to stay.

"If they had come here, I would have given them my own bed," thought Uncle Martin.

He read about the wise men who brought gifts of gold, frankincense and myrrh for the baby Jesus.

"I wouldn't have a gift for Jesus," he thought sadly. But then he caught sight of a tiny pair of shoes he'd made long ago, sitting on the shelf.

"Of course, I would give him those! They are the best shoes I ever made."

Uncle Martin put away the Bible.

That night, he dreamt that somebody came to his room.

"Uncle Martin," said a voice, "you wished to see me and give me a gift. Look for me tomorrow and I will come."

When he woke up on Christmas morning, Uncle Martin knew who had spoken to him. "It was Jesus," he said excitedly. "He is going to visit me!"

He made his morning coffee and then looked out of the window to see if Jesus was coming, but all he saw was the road sweeper, shovelling snow in the bitter wind.

"That poor man is shivering," thought Uncle Martin, so he invited him inside to share his coffee. The road sweeper was very grateful. As he warmed his frozen hands, Uncle Martin told him about his dream.

"You are a kind man," said the road sweeper, "I hope your dream comes true."

When he'd gone, Uncle Martin stoked up the fire and went out into the street to see if Jesus was coming. All he saw was a mother and father and two small children, carrying heavy bundles. "Their clothes are too thin for this winter weather," he thought, so he invited them into his house.

"We are refugees," explained the man. "We had to leave our country and now we're travelling to a new home." The mother pulled back the cover of her bundle and there was a baby.

Uncle Martin found some clothes that belonged to his wife and children, then he fetched an old coat of his own for the father to wear. While the family put them on, he told them about his dream.

"You are a good man," the father said. "I hope your dream comes true." When they were about to leave, Uncle Martin remembered the tiny shoes and gave them to the mother for her baby.

All Christmas day, Uncle Martin waited for Jesus. He gave money to the village carol singers and invited a lonely neighbour to share his Christmas meal, but by nightfall, Jesus hadn't appeared.

"So, it was just a dream," he sighed.

Then, suddenly, he was not alone. All the people Uncle Martin had helped that day appeared before him. Each one whispered "Didn't you see me, Uncle Martin?"

"I was cold and you gave me warmth," said the voice he'd heard the night before. "I needed clothes and you clothed me. I was hungry and you fed me."

Then Uncle Martin knew that Jesus had come after all and his heart was filled with joy!

DECEMBER

DECEMBER 25TH
CHRISTMAS

THE LEGEND OF THE POINSETTIAS
A MEXICAN STORY

It was Christmas Eve, but Pepita was sad. There were no decorations in the house where she lived with her grandmother, and there was no money to buy her a present.

"Don't be sad, Pepita," said Grandmother. "Come, give me a kiss. Even the smallest gift from someone who loves you makes you happy."

Pepita kissed her grandmother and hugged her tight.

"Now," said Grandmother, "my old legs won't walk me to Church anymore, but you can go to see the manger where the baby Jesus will lay."

So Pepita took her shawl and set off for the village. On the way she met many people, bringing presents to lay before the manger.

Pepita felt bad that she had nothing to give. When she reached the church she held back, ashamed of going in empty handed.

Then Pepita remembered her grandmother's words. "Even the smallest gift from someone who loves you makes you happy." She looked around but all she could see were weeds growing by the path. Could such a humble gift make Jesus happy? As there was nothing else, she picked a bunch and made a little bouquet and followed the others inside.

When people saw Pepita carrying a little bunch of weeds through the church they stared and whispered, some even laughed.

"That's not a gift to bring to Jesus," they said.

But Pepita walked bravely on.

To her astonishment, as she came near to the manger, the green leaves started to turn red. Everyone fell silent and watched in wonder. Step by step, the weeds blossomed until Pepita's arms were filled with beautiful scarlet star-shaped flowers. Pepita smiled with joy. She laid the flowers between the ox and the ass, making a bright garland around the manger.

Then everyone came forward to light a candle, for they felt they had seen a miracle.

When she left the church that Christmas night, Pepita's heart was singing. Beside the path lay one red poinsettia flower that must have fallen from her arms. Pepita picked it up and hurried home to give it to Grandmother.

DECEMBER 26TH
KWANZAA

THE FEAST
AN AFRICAN STORY

A chief decided to have a great gathering of his people. He sent a messenger to spread the word in every village.

"You are all invited to a great gathering at the Chief's house," said the messenger. "The Chief will provide a splendid feast for everyone and he asks that each man brings a gourd of palm wine to add to the pot."

When they heard this, all the people were excited. There was much talk in the villages about what delicious food would be served at the feast.

On the morning of the great gathering, everyone dressed in their best clothes.

"You look very fine!" said one woman to her husband. "Now, fill a gourd with palm wine to take with us."

"But we don't have any," said her husband.

"Then you must hurry and buy some," replied the woman.

The man frowned. "Why should I have to spend money when the feast is free?" he complained.

"We must make a contribution, like everyone else," said his wife.

Her husband smiled. "If everyone is making a contribution, a gourd of water won't be noticed in a big pot of wine!"

And so, despite his wife's protest, he filled his gourd with water.

When they arrived at the feast, the man tipped his contribution into the pot and smiled at his clever trick.

The Chief welcomed everyone and took the first drink.

"My friends," he said solemnly, "I see from the quality of the wine you have brought, how much you value my hospitality."

Then all the guests took a drink — and there was nothing but water in every cup!

A YEAR FULL OF EVENTS

New Year *1st January*
The first day of the year, according to the Gregorian calendar used by most countries. It is often celebrated with fireworks.

Chinese New Year *New moon between 21st January and 20th February*
Also called the Spring Festival. This is the most important Chinese celebration and lasts for fifteen days.

Candlemas *2nd February*
A Christian celebration of Jesus as "the light of the world." On this day candles are blessed in church.

Valentine's Day *14th February*
Once the feast day of St Valentine, since medieval times it has been associated with love and romance.

Shrove Tuesday *Exactly 47 days before Easter Sunday*
The day when people traditionally feasted before forty days of fasting and reflection during Lent. Also called Pancake Day.

St David's Day *1st March*
St David is the patron saint of Wales. On this day people celebrate Welsh culture and often wear a daffodil or a leek.

World Wildlife Day *3rd March*
In 2014 the United Nations established this day to focus on how people and wildlife may live together in harmony.

Purim *14th Adar in the Hebrew calendar*
A commemoration of how a young Jewish woman, called Esther, saved the lives of her people living in ancient Persia.

St Patrick's Day *17th March*
St Patrick brought Christianity to Ireland and is their patron saint. There are many stories associated with him.

World Water Day *22nd March*
A day to focus on the importance of fresh water and how it can best be managed for everyone in the world.

April Fools' Day *1st April*
The origin of this festival is a mystery, but people have enjoyed playing practical jokes on this day for hundreds of years.

Easter *Sunday after the first full moon of the Spring Equinox*
Easter is a Christian festival celebrating the resurrection of Jesus from the dead. People often give painted or chocolate eggs.

World Health Day *7th April*
The World Health Organisation established this day in 1950, to draw attention to important global health issues.

St George's Day *23rd April*
St George is the patron saint of England. According to legend, he fought a dragon to save a princess.

May Day *1st May*
A spring festival celebrating fertility. May Day customs include crowning a May Queen and dancing around a maypole.

Vesak *Variable; for many, it is celebrated on the first full moon in May.*
On this day, Buddhists all over the world honour the birth, the enlightenment and passing of Gautama Buddha.

World Oceans Day *8th June*
The United Nations designates this as a day to celebrate our oceans and take action to protect them.

Ramadan *Ninth month of the Islamic calendar*
During this month, Muslims fast from dawn to dusk. It is a time for charity, prayers and reciting the Quran.

World Music Day *21st June*
This festival was established in France, in **1981**. Free concerts take place all around the world, encouraging people to make music.

Eid ul-Fitr *The end of Ramadan*
This Islamic festival marks the end of the fast that takes place during the holy month of Ramadan.

Tanabata *4th July*
Japan's Star Festival, when people hang their wishes up.

St Swithin's Day *15th July*
St Swithin was an Anglo-Saxon bishop. Legend says that if it rains on this day, forty days of rain will follow.

International Day of Friendship *30th July*
The United Nations promotes this day of friendship to inspire peace and increase understanding between communities.

Lammas Day *1st August*
Much older than the traditional Harvest Festival, this is a celebration of the first harvest of the year.

Harvest *Full moon closest to the Autumn Equinox*
A time to give thanks for crops that have been gathered. Customs include weaving corn dollies.

Yom Kippur *10th Tishrei in the Hebrew calendar*
The holiest day of the year for Jewish people, also called the Day of Atonement. It is a thoughtful time to fast and pray.

International Day of Peace *21st September*
Established by the United Nations in **1981** as a day to encourage non-violence and cease-fire around the world.

World Food Day *16th October*
A day promoted by various organisations working to raise awareness of poverty and hunger around the world.

Halloween *31st October*
An ancient festival of the dead, now celebrated with many customs, including spooky costumes, trick-or-treating and pumpkin lanterns.

Diwali *15th Kartik in the Hindu lunar calendar*
This festival, observed by Hindus, Sikhs and Jains, is dedicated to the triumph of light over darkness and goodness over evil.

Bonfire Night *5th November*
Also called Guy Fawkes Night. This is a commemoration of a **17th** century plot to blow up the Houses of Parliament in Britain.

Thanksgiving *Fourth Thursday of November in the U.S.A.; Second Monday of October in Canada*
A national holiday in Canada and the U.S.A. It is a time to give thanks for the harvest, often celebrated with turkey and pumpkin pie.

National Tree Week *26th November*
A week of events to promote the love and care of woodland, during which lots of organisations and individuals plant trees.

St Andrew's Day *30th November*
St Andrew is the patron saint of Scotland and many other countries. This day is often celebrated with traditional ceilidh dancing.

Human Rights Day *10th December*
A commemoration of the day the United Nations General Assembly adopted the Universal Declaration of Human Rights.

Christmas *25th December*
The Christian celebration of the birth of Jesus. Also a time of giving gifts, enjoyed by people all over the world.

Kwanzaa *26th December – 1st January*
A week-long African-American festival honouring African culture and heritage.

First published in the UK in 2016 by Frances Lincoln Children's Books, an imprint of the Quarto Group.
The Old Brewery, 6 Blundell Street, London N7 9BH
T (0)20 7700 6700 F (0)20 7700 8066 www.QuartoKnows.com

A catalogue record for this book is available from the British Library.

ISBN 978-1-84780-859-2
eISBN 978-0-71126-125-9

Illustrated with gouache

Edited by Jenny Broom
Designed by Mina Bach
Production by Jenny Cundill
Published by Rachel Williams

Manufactured in Huizhou, China TT062021

3 5 7 9 8 6 4 2

THIS BOOK BELONGS TO:

· ·